PUSHKIN CHILDREN'S

Blue Door Venture

PAMELA BROWN (1924–1989) was a British writer, actor, then television producer. She was just fourteen when she started writing her first book, and the town of Fenchester in the book is inspired by her home town of Colchester. During the Second World War, she went to live in Wales, so her first book, *The Swish of the Curtain*, was not published until 1941, when she was sixteen. She used the earnings from the books to train at RADA, and became an actor and a producer of children's television programmes.

Blue Door Venture

PAMELA BROWN

PUSHKIN CHILDREN'S

Pushkin Press
71–75 Shelton Street
London WC2H 9JQ

Copyright © The Estate of Pamela Brown 2018

Blue Door Venture was first published as in Great Britain, 1949

First published by Pushkin Press in 2018

1 3 5 7 9 8 6 4 2

ISBN 13: 978-1-78269-191-4

Designed and typeset by Tetragon, London
Printed and bound by CPI Group (UK) Ltd, Croydon CR0 4YY

www.pushkinpress.com

Blue Door Venture

NOTES ABOUT THE SETTING

Blue Door Venture was first published in the 1940s, and the following references may require some additional explanation for the modern reader.

Before decimalization in 1971, British currency consisted of pounds, shillings, and pence:

  12 pence = 1 shilling
  20 shillings = 1 pound
  21 shillings = 1 guinea
  so *three and six* means 'three shillings and sixpence'.

The *Blue Door* books were written well before the invention of the mobile phone, and at a time when not everyone had a telephone in their home. Characters in the stories rely on public telephones in order to keep in touch. *Trunk calls* or *trunks* were expensive long-distance phone calls that had to be specially arranged, *wires* were telegrams, dictated over the phone, and a caller who *reversed the charges* was asking the person they were calling to pay for the call.

Woolworth's and Home and Colonial were both department stores.

A rep. (or repertory) company is a theatre company which resides permanently at a particular theatre, regularly changing the performances on offer to their audiences.

A.S.M. is an assistant stage manager.

I

THEATRE COMPANY

'Gosh, it's cold!'

As they turned the corner of Pleasant Street and made for the Blue Door Theatre there was a very wintry gust of wind that made them clutch their scarves tightly round their necks and gasp for breath.

'Yes,' said Nigel, 'I'm afraid we're in for a bad winter. And it can make all the difference to us...'

The Blue Door Theatre had been running for nearly four months, and Fenchester had backed it up splendidly. Most nights of the week the little theatre was nicely full, and on Fridays and Saturdays it was packed as tightly as regulations would allow.

'If only we had a gallery!' Mr Chubb, the elderly business manager, would groan. But expenses were formidable. There were so many items to be considered: salaries, scenery, costumes, posters advertising their shows... Each week the amount left over to share amongst themselves for pocket-money was horribly small.

'You mean,' pursued Jeremy, 'that if we have bad weather so that people stay away, we shan't be able to start paying back the loan the Town Council gave us when we started?'

'Exactly,' said Nigel. 'That's so, isn't it, Mr Chubb?' From deep inside the collar of his overcoat Mr Chubb agreed.

Lyn pulled the hood of her thick coat up over her long dark hair and said thoughtfully, 'But we're sure to do good business at Christmas, aren't we? Especially if we do a pantomime.'

Bulldog scratched his ginger head in a worried manner. 'As far as I can see, it all boils down to the boiler...' The heating system of the theatre was Bulldog's responsibility, and the bane of his life. 'If only it will stop being temperamental, we may be able to keep the temperature up to something fairly comfortable inside the theatre, so that people will still come, if only to keep warm. But if the stove conks out we're done for.'

Outside the theatre they took the key from the usual hiding-place under a brick, and unlocked. Mr Chubb went at once into the tiny box-office and settled himself at the desk with plans of the seating before him. It was cheering to see one or two people already waiting to book seats, even at ten o'clock on a cold December morning.

'Come on,' said Lyn, when the bare rehearsal light on the stage had been switched on. 'Let's get cracking. We'll see if anyone knows anything about Act Two.'

Her brother Jeremy groaned. 'I'm afraid I hardly know a word. I only just seem to have learned the last play.'

'You should thank your lucky stars that we're doing fort-nightly rep., not weekly,' Lyn rebuked him.

They were rehearsing a detective play called *Murder in Mid-Channel*, and it involved many difficult stage falls. By the time

8

they broke for ten minutes for coffee at eleven-thirty, they were all inclined to be stiff and bruised—except Vicky, the dancer, who specialized in that sort of thing. 'It's all a matter of relaxation,' she told them. 'Don't you remember being taught that at the Academy?'

As they sat round the table in the grubby café opposite the theatre, sipping coffee made with tinned milk but which was at least hot, they formed a colourful group. There were the Halfords—the twins, Vicky and Bulldog, red-headed and freckled, and Nigel, their big brother, dark and brown-eyed; Sandra Fayne, fair and frail-looking; Lynette Darwin, dark and striking, and her brother Jeremy in a pale blue sweater that matched his eyes and suited his curly fair hair. And then, of course, Ali, the dark, limpid-eyed Indian boy who had become their stage manager. Myrtle gave a fruity laugh that rang out in the tiny low-raftered room. She was the character actress whom they had met at the Academy. Stout and friendly, she mothered the whole company. Billy, the little assistant stage manager, stammered and stuttered and dropped things in well-meaning confusion, always trying to be helpful and not quite bringing it off. The scenic artist, Terry, was draped as lazily as usual over the table. But despite the lackadaisical manner he affected, and the fact that one never saw him actually working, the sets which he turned out were very often magnificent. Mr Edwin Chubb's white locks added a touch of distinction to the company, and he was never at a loss for some anecdote from his long experience of the theatre with which to amuse them or to prove a point.

The town of Fenchester had grown to love this odd collection of personalities that formed the company of the Blue Door Theatre, especially as the nucleus were local born and bred. But

9

they were interested, too, in the new faces that came and went, when extra artistes had to be called in for shows with large casts. These were usually people who had been at the British Actors' Guild Academy with the Blue Doors.

Just as they were putting their coats on to return to the theatre, a telegram boy stepped inside the door of the café. 'You from the theatre?' he inquired.

'Yes.'

'Well, there's this for you...' He handed the telegram to Nigel.

Be seeing you tonight. Hope you've got a juicy part for me. Maddy, it read.

'Oh, good,' cried Nigel, and read it aloud. Maddy, Sandra's sister, was the youngest member of the company, and was still in the junior school of the Academy, and could only act at Fenchester during the holidays.

'Yes,' said Sandra, 'I meant to tell you we're expecting her home tonight.'

'I'm afraid there's no part for her in this murder thing,' said Nigel, 'but she can help Billy with the noises off.'

'She'll love doing thunder and rain,' said Sandra.

'Yeth, I could do with thome help,' said Billy, 'even if it's only Maddy, I mean—er—'

Nigel laughed. 'Yes. We know what you mean. You'll have to keep an eye on her. But perhaps she won't be so wild, now that she's had to look after herself for a whole term at the Academy.'

By lunch-time it was colder than ever, and their noses were tinged with pink as they hurried home. In the afternoon they rehearsed with their coats on, and Bulldog had a long session with the stove, stoking it up ready for the evening performance of *The Rivals*. 'I declare this thing is human,' he announced.

'Whenever it's preparing to be really infuriating, it makes horrid little chortling noises.'

As it was Thursday night, and the fifth time they had performed *The Rivals*, there were no worries as to the evening's show, and they were able to have large and leisurely high teas. Conveniently, the new members of the Blue Doors had managed to find digs in the road where the others lived, so they were able to go to and from the theatre in a noisy laughing arguing gang.

Just before time for the curtain, Maddy arrived. There was a violent banging on the little stage door at the back of the building, and when they opened it, there she was, as plump and untidy and grinning as ever.

'Hallo, you stooges!' she cried. 'I'm back. And am I glad!' She was surrounded by numerous pieces of luggage, including a parcel done up in newspaper that was beginning to split open, displaying a hot-water bottle and a rather grubby pair of tights.

'Let me in—quickly...' She dragged all her cases in after her, and made a quick tour of the dressing-rooms and the stage, greeting everyone. Then she had a peep through the curtains to survey the audience who were coming in by this time. Nigel hastily dragged her back.

'That we do not allow,' he said firmly. 'It's the most amateur thing in the world to see a bulge appear in the tabs, and an eye glued to the gap.'

'Sorry,' Maddy apologized sunnily. 'I can't get used to the idea of us being so fiercely professional.'

'Clear stage, *please*,' yelled Ali, as he did a last minute tour of inspection to see that the furniture and properties were in their right places.

Maddy hurried round to the front of the theatre to watch the show. Mr Chubb greeted her by intoning, 'Hail to thee, blithe spirit—'

'Hail to thee, too,' replied Maddy. 'Can I have a comp., please?'

Mr Chubb frowned. 'On what grounds, may I ask, do you wish for a complimentary seat?'

Maddy giggled. 'Well, I'm in the business, too.' Laughing, he gave her a ticket for the front row of the stalls. Throughout the show she kept her ears skinned for remarks from the audience. And all that she heard was very cheering.

'Oh, I come every other Thursday night. Have my seat booked regular...'

'Yes, I wouldn't miss a show for anything...'

'Good, this time, isn't it?'

'Yes, well, they always are. Clever, you know, aren't they?'

Maddy sat glowing inwardly with pride, but outwardly inclined to shiver, for the theatre could not be called warm by any stretch of imagination. Bulldog's stove made quite a lot of busy crackling noises, especially during the quieter scenes, but did not throw out a lot of heat. Several people in the audience recognized Maddy and came and chatted to her in the interval, and she had a delicious feeling of being back where she belonged and of being appreciated. When the last scene of the Restoration comedy had been brought to a graceful close, and the cast had taken their bows, Maddy went round again, and sat in the girls' dressing-room, chattering sixteen to the dozen and getting in everyone's way.

'... And then I came top in fencing, because everyone else was so bad, but, on the other hand, I came bottom for ballet—'

'Maddy, dear, you're standing on the hem of my dress. Do you mind?'

'Sorry—because I'm always fooling about at the back of the class, you see—'

'Maddy, can I have that chair? I want to get my make-up off.'

'Yes, of course—and, you see, Madame is awfully hot on that sort of thing, and—'

'Wouldn't you like to go and help Ali set the stage for tomorrow's rehearsal, dear?' said a tactful Sandra eventually.

'Goodness, it's like having a tame whirlwind in the dressing-room,' said Lynette when Maddy had gone. But it gave them all a nice sense of completeness to have her back again.

'Christmas should be fun,' said Vicky, for no reason whatsoever.

The next morning at coffee-time they discussed their Christmas plans, and decided to do 'Goldilocks and the Three Bears' and to write the script themselves.

'It will save us paying author's fees,' said Nigel. 'I think it's an unusual choice, too. Maddy can play Goldilocks, and have her hair out of pigtails, in nice fat ringlets.'

Maddy exclaimed in horror, 'Preserve me! I'd much rather play the smallest bear.' She squeaked sadly, 'Who's been sitting in *my* chair?' making the waitress nearly drop the coffee she was placing on the table.

'No, you'll have to play Goldilocks, and Billy can be the little bear.'

Billy blushed with pleasure. Usually he wasn't allowed to act because of his stutter and lisp.

'Myrtle can be the medium size bear, and Nigel the big bear,' they planned, and then began to try to think of jokes and songs for the script.

'And we can have half a dozen of your little Academy friends down to play fairies or robins or something,' Nigel said to Maddy.

'You must give me the names of some who can dance. We'll just pay their expenses, and they can do it for the sake of getting experience. We can give them a few shillings pocket-money if you like.'

Mr Chubb, always with an eye to business, said to Nigel, 'You know, dear boy, it's going to be an expense hiring the skins for the bears.'

'Oh, we needn't hire,' cried Sandra. 'If we can buy masks I can run up the rest of the bears on the machine.'

'Poor bears!' laughed Maddy. 'Oh, I'm getting terribly excited about it.' She stirred her coffee with such abandon that it splashed and made the table-cloth even dirtier.

'Well, we've still got this murder thing to get on before we can start rehearsing the panto,' said Nigel, 'but we must write as much of it as we can this week and next, so everyone set to and try to get ideas.'

All that week they went round scribbling on pieces of paper and backs of envelopes and reading out verses and gags to each other, saying, 'Do you think that's funny? No, perhaps not...'

And it got colder and colder. On the first night of *Murder in Mid-Channel* it started to snow. Just at the time when people should have been setting out for the show, it began... first of all a few harmless little snow-flakes... then more and more, until the sky was full of them, busily whirling down, to coat the streets and the buildings of Fenchester, and make its population firmly determined to stay away from the theatre that night.

Mr Chubb, sitting freezing in the box-office, counted the people going in, and it didn't take long. In his moth-eaten astrakhan-collared overcoat, and wrapped in a travelling rug, he counted the takings, the smallest by far that they had ever had. He clucked his tongue, and looked at the booking plan for the week. It was sparse in the extreme.

Going home that night after the show, remembering the thin applause of the few people in the house, and the hollow echoing of their voices in the half-empty theatre, the Blue Doors were more depressed than they had ever been since the theatre opened. Up till now, snow had been the signal for great rejoicing—for the bringing out of toboggans and greasing of skates. But now all that sort of thing seemed a very long way behind, and the snow was a danger and a menace to them.

'It won't be much,' said Bulldog without conviction. 'Look, it's slacking off a bit now. It'll all be gone by tomorrow.' But the flakes continued to fall, daintily, yet relentlessly. Maddy threw a snow-ball rather guiltily, and everyone looked at her as though she had committed a crime.

'Sorry,' she said. 'I wanted to relieve my feelings.'

'If your feelings need any relief tomorrow morning,' Bulldog said, 'come down to the theatre early and help me to shovel some coal under cover out of the yard. It'll be hopelessly wet.'

Next morning, directly after breakfast, Maddy, in a balaclava helmet, wellingtons and a sleighing suit, made her way to the theatre through the deep crisp snow. It was really rather lovely, she had to admit, the old town covered in a white garment, but *would* they get any audience that night? Every morning during the next couple of snowy weeks she was down at the theatre early, helping Bulldog with the stove and madly shovelling coal. Until one morning, after the opening of *Murder in Mid-Channel*, he met her at the door of the theatre looking a little strange. His face was so pale that the freckles on it stood out sharply.

'Oh, Maddy,' he said weakly, 'the stove's gone wrong.'

2

COLD COMFORT

All the morning they wrestled with the stove. Rehearsal had to go by the board. It was more important that they should have a reasonably warm theatre for the evening performance. Clouds of black smoke filled the hall, and there were terrifying roarings and gurglings from the stove, but no heat whatsoever. Nigel dashed out to try to get a workman to come and look at it, but it was impossible.

'What on earth shall we do?' said Sandra. 'There's no hearth, even, where we could make a fire—nothing.'

Nigel said firmly, 'We'll all have to bring electric fires from home and plug them into the lights. We've got two that I can bring. What about you?' he asked the Darwins.

'One, I think,' said Jeremy.

'No,' contradicted Lyn. 'It's fused.'

'We've got one,' said Sandra, 'but it doesn't throw out much heat.'

'Well, they'll have to do for tonight,' said Nigel, 'and tomorrow we *must* get the stove mended.'

'Now for goodness sake let's start rehearsing this awful pantomime,' said Lyn. 'All the fairies and robins and things are arriving tonight, aren't they, Maddy? So we must have some sort of idea of the show.'

'Yes,' said Maddy. 'Three of them are coming tonight, and three tomorrow morning.'

'Oh, dear, and I haven't worked out their dances at all,' groaned Vicky.

'Never mind,' comforted Maddy, 'just tell them to flit.'

It was very difficult to be bright and debonair in the pantomime tradition on that ice-cold stage, wearing so many clothes that they looked like Tweedledum and Tweedledee. They had introduced a prince and Goldilocks' elder sister into the original story and these were played by Vicky and by Sandra. Lyn and Bulldog played Goldilocks' mother and father, and Jeremy was the Demon King, who spoke the Prologue and Epilogue. Altogether it was an amusing mixture of the traditional and the topical. But all the time they rehearsed, they were wondering what it would be like playing in flimsy clothes in the ever-lowering temperature. Already they had got colds in various stages, and lines were somewhat muffled with cough sweets, and top notes had to be taken as sung.

During the afternoon rehearsal Mr Chubb poked his nose round the door and called out, 'You'd better be good this evening. Mrs Potter-Smith has just rung up and booked three seats.' They groaned expressively.

'Is that woman still alive?' demanded Maddy.

17

'Very much so,' Jeremy told her. 'She wrote to the papers when we did *On the Spot* complaining that a play all about gangsters "wasn't healthy".'

'Give me a gangster any day, rather than that old hag.'

'She *would* be coming tonight! Not only is it a murder play, and she'll be sure to take exception to that, but we haven't got any proper heating. Oh, confound the woman—Come on, let's go and have tea.'

As they trudged home, Lyn said despondently, 'Why on earth do we do it? In any other job we'd have finished for the day by this time, and could sit in front of fires and eat our evening meal at a reasonable hour—'

'Well, why *do* we do it?' demanded Nigel. 'If you don't like it, I should give it up. There are a dozen attractive and capable girls that I can think of this moment who would be willing to step into your shoes.'

'Oh, shut up,' laughed Lyn. 'I was only having a nice grumble.'

The extra electric fires were duly plugged in that evening, and as soon as the footlights were switched on five minutes before the curtain should have gone up, the whole system fused, the load being too heavy. There was total darkness for about ten minutes, while Bulldog and Ali stumbled about trying to put things to rights, and the audience twittered nervously. Above the twittering came Mrs Potter-Smith's unmistakeable voice, 'Oh, dear... this darkness... so trying... and the cold... what a *pity* they can't run things more efficiently. But there, of course, the poor dears... we can't expect much, can we... so young... Oh, it's so cold...'

At last the lights were put right and the curtain was able to go up. The play was a very ordinary thriller, the sort of thing they sometimes threw in to try to appeal to popular taste. Most of the audience loved it, and in the cheaper seats they 'Oohed' and 'Ahhed' at the exciting bits, but Mrs Potter-Smith's disapproval became more and more vocal as the cold attacked her toes and nose. Her offended cluckings and disapproving sniffs punctuated the whole performance. Occasionally, for good value, she threw in an audible shiver.

'She needn't think it's any too warm on stage, either,' said Vicky in the interval. The dressing-rooms were icy too, as the electric fires had been sacrificed for the auditorium.

'Act Two, please,' shouted Ali.

'Yes,' said Nigel, 'and let's speed it up so that we can get home and get warm.' The rest of the play moved so quickly that it was rather like an early film being projected too quickly. People died off at an incredible rate and at last the stage was littered with corpses, the intrepid detective, played by Nigel, had discovered the murderer, and the curtain came down.

'Gosh!' cried Maddy, 'my arm aches from turning the handle of that wind machine. It didn't make me any warmer though.'

From the imitation wind and rain of the theatre, the audience turned out into the only too real blizzard that was blowing outside.

Just as the company were preparing to lock up the theatre for the night, Mr Chubb appeared, shepherding three small and shivering girls.

'Look what I've found,' he said. 'Three snow-fairies...' They looked a pathetic sight, with snow caked all round their faces and on their shoulders and shoes. They didn't look at all happy. In fact, the lower lip of the smallest of them was trembling slightly. Maddy rushed to greet them excitedly.

'Hallo, Buster! Hallo, Snooks!' she cried, and they brightened up immediately. While they were being introduced, Vicky suddenly clapped her hands together loudly.

'Yes, of course...' she cried. Everyone looked at her, and she hastened to explain. 'I've been absolutely stuck for what sort of dances to have in the pantomime, but—obviously—we must have a snow-flake ballet. Jeremy, quickly, some snow-flake music!'

'Oh, heavens,' grumbled Jeremy. 'Aren't we ever going home?' But he sat down at the piano and improvised some light, dancing, flake-ish music, and Vicky started to dance in the half-lit theatre, making up the steps as she went along. The fairies watched, very impressed, then, as they picked up the idea, shed their sodden coats and scarves and joined in. Maddy was the next to try, galumphing happily round, completely out of time, and bumping into everyone else. Bulldog joined her, and the dancing became more and more eccentric. Then Ali joined in, doing an oriental version of the steps that Vicky was executing. Soon they were all dancing round and round the auditorium, up on to the stage and down again. Mr Chubb was doing a stately *pas seul* in the foyer. At last, Jeremy's fingers gave out, and they all collapsed laughing.

'I'm awfully glad I could come down here,' said the skinny fairy Maddy had hailed as 'Buster'.

Next day things became really bad. People rang up and cancelled bookings for not only that night but the rest of the week also.

'Because I hear the theatre's so cold,' was the usual explanation.

'And who have they heard it from?' demanded Lyn. 'That wretched Mrs Potter-Smith, of course. I'd like to wring her fat neck.'

'I wonder,' said Nigel, 'whether we ought to close down until the weather improves—'

'Impossible, dear boy,' said Mr Chubb. 'We must stay open and try to rake in every penny to cover overhead expenses.'

'This will have to be the cheapest pantomime ever put on,' said Nigel. 'We can't afford to hire a thing. Thank heavens there aren't any author's fees. We'll have to set about repairing old scenery like mad. I hoped for some new pieces—but that's out of the question now.'

'Yes,' agreed Mr Chubb, then cheering up slightly added, 'The panto will bring the crowd in. People will see a show at Christmas, however cold it is. But if only we could get the stove mended—'

Bulldog tore his hair. 'If anyone else mentions the word "stove" I shall start climbing the walls. I've been to everyone I can think of to get it mended, and it's absolutely hopeless for at least a week.'

And by the time the stove was mended the damage was done. Fenchester was determined to stay away as long as the cold weather lasted. Instead of going to the chilly theatre they went to the centrally heated cinemas. Mrs Potter-Smith had certainly done her work well. She had spread word of the iciness of the theatre and the poorness of the show all round the Ladies' Institute, the tea shops and sewing parties. And it was from these sources that most of their audiences came.

The Wednesday matinée had to be cancelled as only three people turned up. Despondently the Blue Doors trudged through the slushy snow and spent the afternoon in the cinema.

'Though why we should swell *their* profits, I don't know,' grumbled Nigel. The film was all about a stock company in

America who nearly went broke and then some dear old gentleman died and left them a lot of money, and also they got the opportunity to do a show on Broadway, which was an instantaneous success. The Blue Doors came out of the cinema laughing hollowly. That evening they played to fifteen who were all in the cheaper seats, and fourteen of them had severe colds.

And so it went on, with the snow and Mrs Potter-Smith both doing their worst. And then, although the snow stayed, Mrs Potter-Smith disappeared. She was not at the meetings of the Ladies' Institute nor the sewing parties. She did not sit in Bonner's devouring sticky cakes at eleven o'clock and tea-time. She did not even go to change one 'nice romantic novel' for another at the lending library. And then the awful news got round. Mrs Potter-Smith was ill. She had got pneumonia. She was in hospital. What is more, she had contracted pneumonia the night she visited the Blue Door Theatre. When the company heard it, they stood and looked at each other, horrified.

'That,' said Jeremy, 'has torn it.'

'Oh, what foul luck,' lamented Nigel. 'I'm sorry the old monster has got pneumonia, but why—*why*, did she catch it here?'

'If she did!' said Maddy sagely. 'She might just as well have caught it at that display of Greek dancing which she and some of her pals gave the other night. Judging by the pictures in the papers they were galumphing about wearing next to nothing.'

'What a horrible thought,' shuddered Jeremy. 'Still, even if she did catch it there, we can't prove it. And the one or two people who might have braved it and come to the theatre will now obviously stay away.'

By the Monday of the second week of *Murder in Mid-Channel* the stove was mended and burning merrily, throwing out a fine heat to all corners of the theatre, and nearly roasting those who were seated near it. And the audience consisted merely of a handful of the Blue Doors' parents and friends, who had all gallantly insisted on paying for their seats.

'It's heart-breaking!' cried Lyn. 'Don't the Fenchester people want a theatre?'

'Evidently not in this weather,' said Sandra, 'and one hardly blames them.'

'Let's—let's put up a notice outside the theatre saying, "It's warm in here",' suggested Maddy.

'No-one would believe us. They'd believe Mrs Potter-Smith,' said Vicky gloomily.

'It *would* come just now, when we've got six extra to pay next week.'

In lieu of some of their meagre pay, the six extra fairies were being lodged free by the parents of the Blue Doors.

'It's awfully sweet of our mothers to do it, you know,' said Nigel. 'We couldn't have afforded any more in the way of salaries. I'm afraid there won't be any for us seven this week, or for some time to come.'

'We just *must* make a success of the pantomime,' was the theme on everybody's lips. It was shaping quite well now. The dances were all planned out, and the lines of the dialogue and the songs nearly learned. Maddy was a dumpy and sensible Goldilocks, and the antics of the three bears would be sure to appeal to children.

It was Maddy who had the best publicity idea concerning the pantomime. One day she came in to rehearsal saying, 'I've got hold of something that may be useful for the panto. Mr Smallgood and Whittlecock is bringing it down in a few minutes.'

Mr Smallgood (or *was* he Mr Whittlecock?) was the owner of an antique shop bearing those two names that stood at the corner of Pleasant Street. Maddy had often bullied him into lending them things for previous shows. Soon he appeared, bowed under an enormous furry burden. It was a large stuffed brown bear.

'See!' cried Maddy delightedly. 'We can stand him outside the theatre with a notice on him saying, "Come and see me in my starring role", or something like that.' They did so. Bruin stood bravely outside the theatre in the snow, inviting people to come and book for the pantomime. He proved a great favourite with children, many of whom dragged their parents in to the box-office to get seats for Christmas week.

'Oh, yes,' Mr Chubb reassured the inquiring mothers, 'we're all fitted up for this sort of weather now. Snug as anything with a new heating system.' And, suppressing a shiver, he would hand over the tickets.

One evening after the show Nigel called an emergency meeting of the seven original Blue Doors and Mr Chubb. 'We must discuss economy,' he said. 'How can we save money, apart from not having any salaries ourselves?'

'And making our own costumes,' added Sandra, whose fingers were sore with sewing.

'We could do all classical plays for a bit,' suggested Lyn, 'and save royalties.'

Maddy giggled. 'We'll have old Bill Shakespeare turning in his grave and demanding author's fees.'

'Yes, that would be one thing,' agreed Nigel, ignoring the interruption. 'But then that would mean difficult historical costumes.'

'We'll cope,' sighed Sandra. 'We always used to when we were amateurs—never hired a thing, and I'm sure the costumes weren't worse than hired stuff.'

'Well, what else is there?' demanded Nigel.

'What about letting the theatre occasionally for amateur shows,' suggested Bulldog.

'No, they mostly go to the Ladies' Institute Hall. They don't have to pay for that.' They racked their brains in silence as they sat in conclave in the girls' dressing-room. Then there came a tap at the door. It was Buster, the smallest fairy.

She blushed and faltered and said, 'Well, we couldn't help knowing, me and the other fairies, that is, that the theatre is hard up. Maddy told us. We haven't been listening. So we thought we'd like to say that we don't want to take our pocket-money—'

She was drowned by the reactions of the Blue Doors. Vicky burst into tears, Maddy thumped her on the back, Sandra and Nigel said, 'But of *course* you must be paid,' and Jeremy and Bulldog roared with laughter; and when she had bolted out of the room again Lyn said slowly, 'Funny how something always turns up to show that life is worth living...'

25

3

SNOW-FLAKE BALLET

'ONE—TWO—THREE, one—two—three,' chanted Vicky. 'Buster, your knees are bent. Snooks, smile, please. Eyes and teeth—that's right.' The snow-flake fairies twirled and arabesqued round the tiny stage. 'They're going to be the best bit in the show,' Vicky whispered to Lyn, who was sitting beside her in the stalls.

'I think you've trained them awfully well,' said Lyn, 'and they'll take up a nice lot of time. The show is very short, you know. Our ingenuity doesn't stretch very far.'

'That's lovely, dears,' said Vicky, when they had finished. 'Thanks, Jeremy. That accompaniment is fine now.'

It was only a few days to the opening of the pantomime, and the way that the bookings were piling up gave fresh enthusiasm to their rehearsals. The weather had settled down into a hard crisp frost, with the snow still on the ground. It was easier to get about and the cold did not seem so penetrating. They had sent out posters and handbills to all the villages in the surrounding district, hoping that the country people would be lured to Fenchester by the magic word 'pantomime', and it seemed that their efforts were to be rewarded.

On the Sunday before the opening Monday, the theatre was a hive of activity. There was the previous week's set to be taken down, and the basic scenery of the pantomime to be put up. Changes of scene in the pantomime were being effected by curtains and painted back-cloths. Sandra sat at the sewing machine, whirring away and directing the fairies who were sewing on last minute hooks and eyes and press-studs. Nigel and Bulldog, Ali and Billy, had long sessions on the lighting and experimented with coloured gelatines over the spot and footlights, and Jeremy was constantly being accosted with 'Do you mind just running over the last verse of my opening number?'

It was a hard day's work, and at the end of it, when Nigel had announced 'Dress rehearsal ten-thirty tomorrow morning,' they were glad to make for home and supper.

As they neared their gates, Vicky said, 'Oh, Mummy says that anyone who likes can come in for a snack. We've got stacks of sausages, for some unknown reason. If you don't mind eating in the kitchen...' It seemed an inviting idea, and they all piled into the Halfords' kitchen, and fried sausages.

'Maddy!' Bulldog admonished her after her fifth. 'If you eat another sausage you'll look like one.'

'She does already,' said Jeremy, 'so what does it matter?' It was so warm and cosy sitting round the kitchen table swapping stories, that the temptation was to stay there late, but Sandra was firm.

'No, come on, everyone—Maddy, at any rate. We've all got a very hectic day tomorrow—and we can't have fairies with bags under their eyes!'

'Sure you wouldn't like another sausage all round?' inquired Bulldog, eyeing the frying pan.

'Heaven forbid!' cried Jeremy, loosening his belt.

Next morning everyone was down at the theatre as early as possible. Terry was hastily slapping paint on a few last pieces of scenery, and warning people not to brush their clothes against it. Last-minute faults in costumes were discovered as they were put on, and Sandra, bristling with pins, was kept busy altering and taking in and letting out.

Although the dress rehearsal had been called for ten-thirty, it was past eleven by the time they were ready to start.

The set for the first act was the interior of the cottage where Goldilocks and her family lived. Before the curtain went up, Jeremy stepped in front of it in his guise of the Demon King, and started on the prologue. He had just reached the lines:

> You'll see me in a little while
> Wreck their plans with fiendish guile—

when the door at the back of the theatre was flung open. Jeremy faltered and stopped, shading his eyes across the footlights to see who was the intruder.

'Yes?' he inquired politely.

'Oh, er—could I see young Mr Halford, please?' came a falsetto voice.

'Well—er—we're rehearsing. Is it important?'

'Oh, yes—most—exceedingly.'

'Oh, well...' Jeremy sighed wearily, then shouted, 'House lights, Billy! Take the curtain up. Nigel, someone to see you...' He retired to a corner mumbling, 'Why Nigel can't see his wretched girl friends some other time...'

The largest bear lumbered up to the visitor and growled 'Yes?' There was a scream from the gloom, and Nigel shouted, 'Billy, for goodness sake put on the house lights...' They went up and Nigel saw that it was Miss Thropple. At no time was Miss Thropple a pleasant sight, but at eleven o'clock on a cold dress rehearsal Monday, she was more than ever unwelcome. She had lank dark hair, a horse face and a perpetual affected giggle.

'Oh, Mr Halford,' she cooed, 'I work in the Education Office.'

'Yes?'

'And there is something that I think you should know.'

'Yes, Miss Thropple?'

'You are employing this week, I believe, half a dozen little girls who are un-licensed...' Nigel went hot and cold under his make-up. How ever had he neglected to think of that detail? He was silent. On the stage the others stood watching the conversation, trying to overhear and wondering what had caused the interruption. 'That is so, is it not?'

'It is, I'm afraid. It's just that we have not had time to apply for licences for them. I'm sure they will be granted, for they are all over twelve—and after all, this is holiday time. They aren't missing any school hours.'

'Ah, yes, yes,' Miss Thropple raised a finger importantly. 'But that is not the point. It is not legal for them to appear without a specially granted licence, and I happen to know that the Education Officer, the Schools Attendance Officer and the Probation Officer are going to prevent it.'

'But it'll take days to get a licence,' groaned Nigel, 'and we open tonight.'

'Without the little girls, I'm afraid,' added Miss Thropple.

Nigel flared up. 'What business have you got to come here, poking your nose into our business? If the little tin gods at your office want to interfere with us, why don't they do it themselves?'

Miss Thropple bridled. 'Well, indeed—I was only trying to help you. I'm a great friend of Mrs Potter-Smith, you see, and she is always so interested in your endeavours, but of course, as you know, she is so unfortunately in hospital, and when I heard what was going to happen about the licences—' At this point, Maddy, who had crept gradually nearer during the conversation, popped up in between them wearing the little short white Goldilocks' dress and ringlets, and, pointing an accusing finger at Miss Thropple, quoted from the script of the pantomime:

What evil sprite is this I see?
Begone—you cannot frighten me—

Miss Thropple recoiled. 'Well, I've done my best. You are most ungrateful—most ungrateful! But I warn you—you will receive a visit from the Probation Officer just before the show tonight. And he will stop the show, if those poor little girls are made to appear.'

'Poor little girls!' roared Nigel. 'What's poor about them, I'd like to know? They're perfectly happy—look at them! And a great deal healthier than you are, I'd like to bet—'

'You are being most impudent!' Miss Thropple quivered with rage. 'I shall leave you to your fate.' And she swept out of the door, colliding with Mr Chubb, who was coming to see what all the noise was about. When she had gone, Nigel sank into a chair and put his head in his hands.

'Oh, no,' he groaned. 'This is more than I can stand.' The others grouped round him silently.

'Is it us?' said Buster guiltily. Nigel nodded. 'Oh, dear,' she quavered. 'We ought to have told you about licences, but we didn't want to tell you because we were afraid they might not give them to us, and then we couldn't be fairies.'

'I blame *you*, Maddy,' Nigel said bitterly. 'You should have reminded me when we got yours—I didn't dream—I mean, they were at the Academy—'

'All right, blame me,' said Maddy bluntly. 'The point is, what are we going to do?'

'Can't we go on tonight?' said Snooks sadly.

Nigel thought for a long time, then said gently, 'No, I'm sorry, but I don't see how you can. We're in such a precarious state at the moment that we can't afford to risk trouble. We're not in a position to defy the Council, because we're under an obligation to them. We can't afford a court case, or a fine—and we certainly can't risk being closed down altogether. This show has got to make up for all the money we lost on the last one.'

'But Nigel,' said Vicky, 'the show will be about twenty to twenty-five minutes shorter! There's their robin number, as well as the snow-flake one—'

'I can't help it,' said Nigel wretchedly. 'They can't go on until we've applied for the licences and got them. And that might take any length of time. Perhaps even until after the show is off—'

'Oh, no,' cried the dismayed fairies.

'Vicky will have to dance to make up the time,' suggested Bulldog.

'Impossible,' said Vicky. 'The dances all come while I'm changing my costumes. And those principal boy tights and boots take an awful long time—'

'What on earth are we going to do?' groaned Jeremy. 'And how did they find out about it?'

'Somehow,' said Maddy, 'I seem to connect it with Mrs Potter-Smith.'

'Yes,' mused Lyn. 'It seems to bear her stamp.'

'Who is Mrs Potter-Smith?' asked one of the fairies.

'Oh, an awful old dame who is always trying to catch us out,' said Maddy. 'She has very false teeth, and dyes her hair an awful colour.'

'Oh,' said Snooks innocently, 'I think we saw her the first day we were here—'

'What?'

'Yes,' said Buster, 'a funny old woman came up to us outside the theatre and asked us were we members of the company, and how old were we, and all sorts of things—'

'That's her!' cried Lyn. 'And she told her pal Miss Thropple who passed it on to the Education people!'

'I'm glad she's got pneumonia,' shouted Maddy. 'I hope it's double—no—treble—or even—what's the next—quad—rupeddle—'

'Shut up, Maddy. It's no good getting excited about it. The panto will be spoiled without the ballet, that's obvious, but we must just think of something else to fill in twenty minutes.' Lyn looked at her watch. 'The point is, the curtain will be going up in just under eight hours' time, so we've got to think quickly—we've still got the dress rehearsal to get through.'

'Well, we must decide what to do before we start to rehearse.'

The fairies sat down and sadly began to undo their ballet shoes. Then suddenly Snooks said, 'I know what—'

'What?' said everyone else.

'Well, you know the night we came, and Vicky got the idea about the snow-flake dance, and everyone was joining in—'

'Yes?'

'Well, it was awfully funny, wasn't it? Don't you remember how we laughed? At Maddy—and Bulldog and Ali—and everyone? Well, why not do that in the pantomime?'

'You mean—a comedy ballet, instead of a serious one?'

'Yes. Just for a few days, until we get licences.' There was a silence while they thought about it, and then slow smiles of approval appeared on their faces.

'It's an idea,' admitted Vicky. 'I wonder if it would go down?'

'I think it would,' said Nigel, hope returning. He jumped briskly to his feet, 'Come on, let's work on that.' They worked on it all the morning until they were having to stop to double up with laughter and, after snatching a hurried lunch at the café, went right through the show. In order to cheer up the disappointed fairies, Nigel asked them all to sit and watch with pencil and paper and note down their criticisms of the performance, just like real live producers. When they had gone all through despite numerous hitches, there was only just time for Billy to be dispatched to fetch a can of tea and some sandwiches, before the audience began to come in. They seemed to arrive by the dozen. Poor Mr Chubb's fingers ached with marking seats in the booking plan, tearing off tickets, changing money and trying to answer the telephone, all at the same time. But there was a gleam in his eye as he did so.

The usual buzz of anticipation among the audience before the curtain went up was louder than ever tonight because of the large proportion of children. Five minutes before the curtain was due to go up, Mr Chubb emerged from his box-office and, with a proud and firm tread, went outside the theatre carrying a square board. This he stood up against the wall in a prominent position. 'House full' it read. Then he resumed his place and blandly but politely turned away as many would-be patrons as were already inside. Most of them, however, he managed to persuade to book for later in the week. Once he had heard the spatter of applause as the curtain rose, he went outside and stood, legs apart and head high, for a long time in the crisp frozen snow, gloating over the notice, happy in the feeling that it was his theatre as much as everyone else's.

Inside the theatre the show was going splendidly. The children all loved the bears, and the grown-ups cooed over Maddy's angelic Goldilocks.

'If you didn't know her,' remarked her mother to Mrs Darwin, 'you would think that butter wouldn't melt in her mouth.'

Vicky's dancing and Sandra's singing were the most polished things in the show, but the hit of the evening was the 'Snowflakes'. Jeremy parodied his original music for the ballet, and Nigel, Bulldog, Ali and Billy did a shocking *pas de quatre*, with Maddy doing a slightly more correct solo, which was still quite funny.

A rather puzzled Education Officer, sitting in the front row with a friend, murmured, 'Now that's very strange—I understood that they were having a lot of little girls to dance—that wretched Thropple woman wasting my time again...' But he was soon laughing with the rest of the audience.

At the end, after a session of choruses in which the children had all joined heartily, led by the six ex-fairies who were planted in different corners of the theatre, the whole company appeared, coming down the traditional flight of stairs which the boys had constructed themselves at the back of the stage. The closing number was one of Jeremy's efforts, entitled 'Christmas Crackers', during which the whole company with crossed arms pulled crackers, and threw some to the audience. The curtain fell on a festive note, and the audience trooped out to the sound of carols thumped out by Jeremy at the piano. All the others were in a state of collapse on the stage, worn out after the long and hectic day.

Snooks came running round, saying, 'It was the loveliest pantomime I've ever seen. I'm so glad I wasn't in it. It was much more fun *seeing* it.'

Mr Chubb clambered on to the stage waving the box-office returns. 'We're saved!' he cried. 'Tonight has nearly made up for all we lost during the last two weeks. Keep it up, and we'll soon be paying back our debt to the Town Council.' Tired as they were, their noises of relief were enthusiastic.

'Thank goodness we haven't got to rehearse tomorrow,' sighed Nigel. 'I shall stay in bed for hours...'

Wearily they took off their make-up and trudged home, singing the pantomime numbers softly to coax along their heavy feet.

'And no visit from the Probation Officer, or whoever the gentleman may be,' observed Nigel. 'I'll apply for the licences tomorrow, and you'll soon be back in the show, you girls,' he assured them.

Next morning Nigel's 'lie in' was disturbed by a visit from Mr Chubb's landlady. He went down, tousle-headed in his dressing-gown, to see the distressed lady.

'It's Mr Chubb,' she gasped. 'I don't like the look of him. It's bronchitis something chronic—croaking like an old raven, he is. It's that draughty box-office, Mr Nigel. It'll be the death of him, I know.'

'Oh, dear,' said Nigel. 'Wait a few minutes, will you, Mrs Smith, and I'll come round and see him.'

Mr Chubb, propped upright on the pillows, was very pale and gasping for breath. 'I'm sorry, dear boy,' he wheezed. 'Seem to have caught cold, or something. Afraid I'll be off tonight.'

'Don't you worry,' said Nigel. 'You stay there and take it easy. I'll find someone for the box-office.'

He rang up the doctor and asked him to visit Mr Chubb, dispatched Bulldog to hold the fort in the box-office for the time being, and then went to all the employment agencies in the town to search for someone to replace the invalid. All day he tramped round in the snow without success. As he went into the theatre that evening Maddy said brightly, 'Did you enjoy your morning in bed?' and wondered why he glowered at her.

4

ENTER LUCKY

Next day Maddy sat shivering in the box-office, wearily adding up the number of tickets she had sold and trying to make it balance with the amount of money in the cash-box. She had either five shillings too little or five shillings too much, but she couldn't quite work out which. In the middle of the calculations the telephone rang. She snatched it up.

'Is that the theatre?' demanded a voice.

'No, it's the Dogs' Home,' she began, then remembering that it was her business to increase the sale of seats, she said in quite a different voice, 'Oh, yes, this is the theatre.'

'Have you any seats for tonight?'

'Nothing left at all until next Wednesday matinée,' Maddy announced proudly, scanning the seating plan. In these few minutes there was already a queue of several people waiting outside the box-office, and by the time she put down the telephone, there were even more. In the absence of Mr Chubb they had found it necessary to man the box-office in shifts, and even Maddy had to take her turn, despite the incredible muddles that always followed in the wake of her session. As she wasn't in the next show that they would be doing because her holiday from the Academy would be over by that time, it fell to her lot rather often while the others were rehearsing. At eleven-thirty Billy appeared with a mug of tea for her.

'In cathe you're thirthty,' he said.

'Thankth awfully,' said Maddy. 'Oh, I'm sorry, Billy, I mean thanks.' But Billy was quite resigned to having his lisp mimicked, consciously and unconsciously.

For the rest of the morning Maddy yawned and shivered and watched the clock, between answering the phone and handing out tickets. The time until lunch seemed endless. She was studying the booking plan closely, and coming to the conclusion that she must have sold the same seat three times over, when a shadow fell across it. She looked into a pair of the beadiest little black eyes she had ever seen. They were set in a round rosy face, and their owner had sleek black hair plastered to his head with a strongly scented hair cream. His shoulders were padded out to a sharp razor-edge line, and his tie had a racehorse hand-painted on it.

'Hi...' he said laconically.

Maddy eyed him suspiciously. 'Can I help you?' she said.

He surveyed the tiny foyer with a lordly air. 'Nice place you've got here,' he observed.

'We think so,' said Maddy.

'Super.

'H'm. Panto—good draw. Do you do good business the rest of the year?'

'Not all the time,' Maddy said truthfully. 'Not during the cold weather, anyhow.'

'What's a kid like you doing in a box-office?' he wanted to know.

Maddy drew herself up to her height of not quite five feet. 'I am one of the joint directors of the theatre,' she told him, flinging one pigtail airily over her shoulder.

He guffawed. 'You're a caution. Whoever heard of the director of anything working in the ticket-office?'

Maddy pondered. It did seem strange, now that she came to think of it. 'Well, you see,' she started, and soon had told him the whole story of the Blue Door Theatre.

He listened, open-mouthed, chortling in the right places. At the end of it he slapped his thigh and said, 'Well, that's better than the pictures—what a story...'

At this moment three people arrived to buy tickets, and the telephone rang. Maddy snatched the receiver up and laid it on the desk while she dealt with the customers. But before she had finished with them her new acquaintance had entered the tiny office by the side door and was answering the phone for her.

'Blue Door Theatre here,' he announced in a carefully Oxford accent, very different from his usual half-Cockney half-American twang. 'Yes, madam. If you will kindly hold the line one minute, I will see what I can do for you.' He peered over Maddy's shoulder at the plan, then returned to the telephone. 'Boxing Day, did you say? First house? Twenty seats... I can do it in the four-and-sixpennies, but not the three-shillings.'

Maddy turned round amazed. Both the three-shilling seats and the four-and-sixpennies were always the last to go as they were the most expensive, and she knew that there were plenty of three-shillings left.

'Hey—you—' she hissed, but he went blithely on, 'Yes, well, I'm sure you want your girls to have the best on their outing, and especially for pantomime it's nice to be nearer the stage, isn't it? Very well, madam, twenty four-and-sixpennies for you and your girls on Boxing Day, first house. What name is it? Thank you, madam. We shall look forward to seeing you.' And he put the receiver down, his eyes shining like currants in a bun.

Maddy goggled at him. 'But we *did* have some three-shilling ones—'

'Sure you did. And you still have. I sold her twenty four-and-sixes. That's twenty times one-and-six more than *you* would have got. You gotta have a sense of business in the theatre racket.' He put his thumbs inside the armholes of his loud yellow waistcoat and looked round the office. 'It's a shame to make a kid like you stick here all day. Are you in the show tonight?'

'Yes,' said Maddy. 'I'm Goldilocks.'

'Well, why don't you run off and amuse yourself for an hour or two? I'm used to this game. I'll look after the booking for you.'

Maddy shook her head vehemently. 'I wouldn't dream of it. I don't know who you are. Why, I don't even know what your name is—'

He stuck his hand out and shook hers briskly. 'Mine's Lucky. What's yours?'

'Maddy. Why are you called Lucky?'

'Because I am. Nothing I touch goes wrong. Back a horse—it comes in. Buy a raffle ticket—win the goods. Why, it's not safe to play me at tiddlywinks. I been on the business side of this racket quite a lot. Business manager to Red Radcliffe and his

Rhythm Boys—and did they clean it up! Had me own party on the beach at Browcliffe last year—made a packet. Just can't go wrong.' He adjusted his tie modestly.

'Well,' said Maddy, 'we could do with a bit of luck round here, so you can stay and help me if you like, but I can't go off and leave you here alone. The others would kill me.'

'Who's the boss here, anyway?'

'Nigel, I suppose. He's the eldest.'

'H'm. How old is he?'

'About your age.'

'Bunch of kids. Need someone with some experience.'

'Well, we've got Mr Chubb who usually does the box-office but he's about seventy, and he's got bronchitis.'

'Old buffers are no good. You want someone young—with ideas... publicity, that's what you need—'

'That's what I think,' agreed Maddy earnestly, and they spent the rest of their morning with their heads together, discussing outrageous publicity stunts, ranging from parades through the town on an elephant to having Maddy mysteriously kidnapped.

When the others appeared at the end of the rehearsal they stared, amazed, at Maddy's new friend.

'Well,' breathed Sandra, 'Maddy certainly does pick them.'

'I'm Lucky,' he announced, holding out his hand to Nigel. 'You're the boss, I can see that. Nice place you've got here. I been giving your little sister a hand.'

'She's not my little sister,' Nigel said rather shortly, 'and I don't really think she needs any help.'

Maddy began to feel a bit guilty. She could see that they were all suspicious of Lucky, and that once more her knack of making friends with strangers was being frowned upon.

'Nigel,' she said, 'Lucky has just sold twenty four-and-sixpennies for Boxing Day. Some sort of outing, isn't it?'

'Girls Friendly Society or something,' said Lucky.

'They wanted to take three-shilling ones, but Lucky made them take four-and-sixpennies—'

'That was a very good effort, but I'm sure I don't know why you should trouble yourself on our behalf,' said Nigel, too politely.

Lucky laid a confidential hand on Nigel's shoulder. 'Now look, chum,' he said, 'I'm only trying to help you. I think you've done a smashing job of work over this place—but you can't attend to *everything* yourself, now can you? I know this racket, mind, been in it myself, and I know it's pretty tough. What you need is someone to look after the business side for you. Someone with push—and experience.'

'We have a business manager, thank you,' said Nigel coldly. 'He's ill at the moment, but will be back in a few weeks.'

Lucky spread his hands. 'Then what's wrong with me taking over temporarily, say?'

Nigel looked at him hard, then, catching the doubting glances from the others, and a warning dig in the ribs from Lyn, said, 'No, I'm sorry. We couldn't possibly take you on without references and testimonials and things, and by the time all those were taken up, Mr Chubb would be back again.'

'O.K.—O.K....' Lucky shrugged his shoulders, smiling and unruffled, 'I can get better jobs elsewhere.'

As he turned to go Nigel said casually, 'Of course, if you're going to be around over Christmas, you can drop in and help Maddy or whoever is in the box-office—just to pass the time. But we can't pay you anything.'

'I'll think about it,' he sang out, hitching the padding in his shoulders into position as he swaggered out into the street.

When he had gone, 'Maddy!' they cried.

'That *awful* boy!' said Sandra. 'Fancy letting him into the box-office! You're not safe to be left alone for five minutes.'

'I didn't let him in,' said Maddy in injured tones, 'he just came in.'

'What a nerve!'

'But you must admit he did a nice piece of work with the Girls Friendly Society or whatever it was.'

'Yes,' said Nigel doubtfully. 'It's more than any of us would have done—or Mr Chubb, come to that. If Mr Chubb thinks people really want to see the show, and can't afford the expensive seats that are left, he's inclined to let them in free to stand at the back. I've caught him at it.'

Lyn said, 'Of course, that awful type was quite right. We do want someone young, with some push—we're all too busy, and Mr Chubb is too nice—'

'But not *that* boy,' said Sandra. 'Not with that suit, and that hideous tie.'

'Snob,' said Maddy. 'You don't look so hot this morning, yourself.'

Sandra surveyed herself in the long mirror in the foyer. Certainly in her faded blue slacks and old school mackintosh, with her hair tied up in a scarf, she didn't present as smart an appearance as Lucky. She sighed. 'Granted. Oh, I expect he meant well. But let's hope he won't turn up again.'

That evening Lucky bought a seat in the front row of the stalls that someone had returned at the last minute. He led the applause at the end of every number, and joined loudly in the choruses. From the stage the Blue Doors could see his shining hair and laughing beady eyes. They raised their eyebrows, but they had to admit that he made the audience even more responsive than usual.

Next morning he was waiting outside the theatre, and helped Nigel and Bulldog take down the new shutters, unlock the box-office and hang out the photos of the show and the artistes.

'A smashing little panto you've got,' he told them. 'Nothing spectacular, but it's got what it takes. Topical and—intimate, I'd call it. That's what I'd call it—intimate. And that Maddy's a caution. And that comedy ballet dancing.'

'We've got some real ballet dancers in the show tonight. Some little kids,' Nigel told him. 'Their licences only came through today.'

'That'll be a draw,' observed Lucky. 'All the old ladies love a few nippers in the show to coo over.' He followed them into the box-office and answered the phone several times, and began persuading people who rang up vainly trying to book for the pantomime, to take tickets for the following show. 'It's another grand Christmas presentation,' he told them suavely. Bulldog and Nigel rocked with silent laughter. When he had put the phone down he turned to them. 'Why, what's wrong with that?' he inquired innocently.

'We're doing *Granite*,' they roared.

'Oh. Isn't that a Christmas show?'

'Er—no. Not really.'

'Then you're crackers. Why not cash in on the Christmas racket? You ought to run that panto a few more weeks. You could have booked it up twice over already.'

44

Nigel and Bulldog looked at each other. It was an idea. It was straying from their usual repertory system of a different show every fortnight, but it would save them a lot of work, and give them more time in which to rehearse *Granite*. Nigel thought quickly, then said, 'Look, Lucky, run round to the printers, will you, it's in the High Street, Bramwell's, opposite the Town Hall, and ask them to print some slips to go over the posters saying, "Retained for another fortnight by popular request".'

'O.K., Chief!' and Lucky was off like a shot.

Nigel and Bulldog looked at each other and grinned sheepishly. 'He's not really a bad chap,' said Nigel casually.

For the rest of the morning while the others rehearsed *Granite*, and Maddy looked after the box-office, Lucky was dashing about on errands continually, to the newspaper office with announcements of the retaining of the pantomime, to the Town Hall for final arrangements about licences, to the post office for stamps—in fact, all the little errands that took up so much valuable time in the running of the theatre. By the end of the day they were wondering how they had ever done without him.

That evening he said to Nigel, 'What do you do about the box-office during the show?'

'We have to close it now that Mr Chubb is away and we're all busy on stage.'

'That's a wicked shame. Wicked. All the people who work during the day don't have a chance to book. And you've got another two weeks of panto to book now.'

'O.K.,' said Nigel. 'You take over. You know how it works already, don't you?'

'Leave it to me,' said Lucky, 'I've worked a box-office before now.' He slapped Nigel on the back, and then, answering the phone, sold the two worst seats in the house to Miss Thropple. They were almost behind a pillar, and most people had learned to fight shy of them. Nigel shook his head in amused wonderment, and went back-stage to change into his bearskin.

From that moment, Lucky took over. He worked like a slave in the box-office, keeping it open from early morning until after the show at night. He got Billy to fetch his meals on a tray from the café, and refused to leave his post for anything. Within a couple of days he had booked up the two remaining pantomime weeks, and was trying to persuade Nigel to run it twice nightly.

'No,' said Nigel. 'It would be too hard on the artistes, especially the kids.'

'But think of the dough you'd rake in.'

Nigel said slowly, 'But we're not doing this for money, you know.'

Lucky laughed cynically. 'Not in it for money! That's a good one! But even if you weren't—you've got debts, haven't you? To the Town Council or something?'

'That's right,' said Nigel. 'We *do* want to get that loan paid off.'

Eventually Lucky persuaded him to put on some extra matinées, to encourage parents to bring small children.

Christmas passed in a whirl of work. They did two shows on Christmas Eve, and two on Boxing Day, and on Christmas Day did excerpts from the show at a neighbouring orphanage. Lucky highly disapproved of this.

'Throwing yourselves away,' he commented. 'Why, they might have brought the whole orphanage to the theatre, if you hadn't been so darned charitable.'

He was so jealous for the financial side of the theatre, that the others found it hard to understand.

'It's not even as if he's getting anything out of it himself,' observed Nigel.

After a while, Nigel felt that he must pay him a small wage for all his hard work, and this Lucky accepted with an airy, 'Thanks, boss. But you needn't've bothered. I got my own income y'know.'

Mr Chubb, still in bed with flannel round his throat, gloated over the accounts. 'By the end of the panto, old laddy, we'll be square—paid off—able to look the world in the face...' he told Nigel. 'I'm so glad. But sorry not to be on the spot while things are so promising.'

Nigel had not told him how much of it was due to Lucky's enterprise, but had merely said that they were managing between them in his absence with the help of a young boy who had turned up.

'Now that we shall have paid off our debt to the Council we can start spending a bit on the shows.' Nigel and Mr Chubb went off into a long pipe dream about new sets and hired costumes and guest artistes down from London, until they were interrupted by Mr Chubb's landlady bringing him his medicine.

As Nigel left, Mr Chubb said, 'Well, dear boy, I shall be back in harness shortly, so keep things humming, won't you?'

Nigel promised he would, mentally adding, 'Or rather, Lucky will,' and left the old man to his cough mixture and back numbers of The Stage.

That night in the boys' dressing-room Nigel said, 'I think we ought to throw a party on the stage on the last night of the pantomime.'

'Oh, yes.' they all agreed. 'Whom shall we invite?' The list grew steadily longer. Their parents, the Town Council, the Bishop, several of the local shopkeepers who lent them properties...

'But the guest of honour,' said Bulldog, 'will most certainly be friend Lucky.'

'But what worries me,' said Nigel, 'is what to do with him when Mr Chubb comes back.'

That, indeed, was a problem.

5

A SENSE OF BUSINESS

'I shall be quite sorry when the pantomime is over,' said Lynette, as she made up in the girls' dressing-room. 'It's been such fun.' Snooks and the other fairies agreed whole-heartedly.

'I wish we hadn't got to go home,' said Snooks, half in and half out of her ballet frock. 'Couldn't we stay on until it's time to go back to the Academy?'

'I'm afraid not,' said Lyn. 'Besides, your mothers will want to see a bit of you during the holidays, won't they?'

'Only two more nights of Goldilocks,' observed Maddy.

'Ouch!' for Sandra was combing out her pigtails and twisting them into ringlets. 'Then I'll be more noises off in *Granite*, then back to London—oh, dear—'

'Isn't it a *relief*,' said Vicky, 'now that we're doing good business. It was such a worry before Christmas when everything was so dreadful. Now it seems just like when we were doing odd shows for fun.'

'"Odd" was the word. Do you remember some of the extraordinary plays we did that we wrote ourselves? Why, we all but made them up as we went along...'

Until 'Beginners, please' was called, they amused the new additions to the company with stories of their amateur days.

The party on the closing night of the pantomime was to be an imposing affair. Nigel announced that the company was to wear evening dress, and the catering was being done by Bonner's, the best restaurant in the town. 'After all,' they kept saying, 'we can afford to splash out a bit now.'

The pantomime became a bit rowdy and farcical, and there were a lot of new lines put in on the last night, and the whole cast were inclined to be giggly, but the audience, a lot of whom were seeing it for the second time, were sympathetically disposed and joined in the fun. The three bears even went down into the audience and gave the children rides. They took six curtains afterwards, and then began frantic preparations for the party.

Trestle tables were laid out on the stage, and loaded with luscious eatables by the four helpers from Bonner's, and the tip-up seats were moved in long rows from the centre of the room to the sides by the whole company, still in their costumes. Then they hurried to change into evening dress and to modify the brightness of their stage make-up. Hardly had they done so, when the guests began to arrive. At the door the company greeted them smilingly, and led them to the buffet.

'This will do us a lot of good in the town,' murmured Lyn to Vicky. 'Watch me being sweet to the Mayor...' and approaching him she treated him to her sweetest smile, and a greeting of 'How glad we are that you were able to come! And you must be such a busy man...'

Lucky, in a white double-breasted dinner jacket, was introduced to everyone as 'our friend who has been helping us on the business side', and he behaved beautifully. He didn't slap anyone on the shoulder or affect his Brooklyn accent, and even had a long conversation with one of the Town Council on the subject of the theatre's finances.

'Now you're a business man yourself,' Jeremy overheard him saying, 'and you know that in this racket, you've gotta have a sense of business...'

Maddy and the fairies were having a wonderful time. They had been told to keep on the clothes they wore in the show, as they were as good as party dresses, and they skipped about in their little short skirts, with everyone making a terrific fuss of them.

Nigel had a long talk with the Mayor, and assured him that they would now be able to repay the loan.

'We could do it tonight,' he said. 'We've got all the takings for the pantomime locked up in the box-office, but perhaps we won't mix business with pleasure.'

'My dear young man, please don't trouble yourself about it. There is absolutely no hurry. You will be repaying it long before we expected.'

'I know,' said Nigel. 'But we want to, so that all the people on the Council who said that they'd never see the money back, will have to eat their words. By the way, how is Mrs Potter-Smith?'

'Recovering, I believe,' smiled the Mayor. 'I'm afraid she'll be up in time for the next Council meeting...' They laughed ruefully.

About midnight, Nigel called for silence and said, 'And now, ladies and gentlemen, we have a few little New Year gifts to present. The Lady Mayoress...' and Snooks ran forward with a large bouquet, and presented it with a careful curtsey.

'And to those snow-flake fairies who have graced us with their presence for the last few weeks...' Maddy, grinning broadly, presented to each of her six friends a celluloid doll dressed up in a white paper ballet skirt. On Buster's she pencilled a beard and moustache, and everyone wondered why the smallest fairy was suddenly stricken with giggles.

'And, lastly, to the gentleman who has brought us so much good fortune and really lives up to his name—Lucky, where are you?' Maddy ran into the middle of the room with another celluloid doll dressed up in a gaudy tie, sitting in a cardboard box with a window cut in it to look like a box-office.

'Lucky, where are you?' shouted Nigel again, but he did not appear. 'Give it to him later, Maddy,' he said. 'Carry on, everyone. It isn't nearly bedtime yet.'

Jeremy sat down at the piano and began to play old and new tunes, and soon everyone was grouped round the piano singing.

It was easy for Nigel to slip away from them unobserved and go to the telephone back-stage. He rang the digs where Lucky stayed and spoke to the landlady. 'I'm a bit worried about Lucky,' he said. 'He seems to have left the party early. I hope he's not ill.'

'Oh, he's not here, Mr Halford,' was the reply. 'Said he was going away for the week-end, but would be back on Monday. I hope he will, I'm sure; he hasn't paid his rent this week, and I see he's took most of his luggage with him.'

'I see. Thank you. I didn't know he was going away this week-end. Sorry to have troubled you at this late hour.' Nigel rejoined the party who were singing 'Begone, Dull Care'.

It was getting on for one o'clock when the guests began to depart. The fairies were all blinking and rubbing their eyes, and Maddy was unashamedly asleep in a chair, with a half-eaten bun clutched in one hand. The caterer's assistants had departed with promises to come in and put things to rights on Monday, and the Town Councillors were ringing up for taxis to take them home.

'You look tired, Nigel,' said Lyn. 'Feel it?' Nigel stared straight through her. 'What's the matter?' Nigel shook his head and walked off.

Lyn shrugged her shoulders and started helping Councillors' wives on with their fur coats. After all the guests had departed (their parents with last-minute instructions 'not to hang around, but to come home as quickly as possible') they made weak attempts to tidy up a bit, and Maddy awoke and started on another snack.

As Lyn was stacking glasses Nigel approached her again and said softly, 'Lyn—I'm frightened—'

She looked up amazed. 'What on earth of?'

'It's—Lucky. He's left his digs without paying the landlady. Said he was going away for the week-end. He didn't tell us that, did he? And he disappeared from the party without a word—'

Lyn said slowly, 'And you think...' She stopped. It was too awful to go on.

'Yes,' said Nigel. 'I feel terrible for thinking it, because if it's nothing of the sort I shall feel ashamed for the rest of my life, when he's done so much to help us.'

'Well, we must go and see,' said Lyn, still in a low voice, so that the others should not hear.

'That's why I'm frightened,' said Nigel; 'in case it's gone.'

'Oh, Nigel!' said Lyn tremulously. They stood staring at each other, unable to move.

'Come on, you loons. What's the matter?' asked Bulldog, who was all ready to go home. 'Surely you haven't just discovered that you're soul-mates after all these years?'

Nigel and Lyn were too sick at heart to retaliate.

'You go on.'

'No, we'll wait for you,' said Vicky, sinking into one of the theatre seats with her tired feet up on the back of another.

Lyn and Nigel fussed about, tidying up, hoping that the others would go, but still they stayed, yawning and nattering. At last Nigel said, 'Come on. We mustn't be cowards and put it off any longer. We must go and investigate. It's all in the box-office. The whole of the pantomime takings. I kept on at him to take it to the bank.'

'And he wouldn't.'

'He would never leave the box-office for long enough.'

Lyn said firmly, 'Come on,' and led the way to the box-office.

'It's locked up all right,' shouted Bulldog after them. 'I checked.'

Nigel produced the keys and unlocked the door. Before he switched on the light, Lyn prayed hastily, 'Please don't let it be true...' But when the light was switched on, it was.

The large cash-box that had been stuffed with notes and silver was lying empty on the desk. For several minutes they stood like statues, then Lyn gave a shuddering groan. Nigel leaned up against the wall, feeling sick, then said very quietly, 'What on earth shall we do?'

'Phone the police, I suppose,' said Lyn dully.

'Oh, how could he! Don't let's tell the others... We're done for... Oh, Lyn...' Nigel was incoherent with distress. A soft footfall behind them made them look up—a new hope springing in them—but it was only Vicky, her green eyes full of curiosity.

'Whatever...' she began, then saw the cash-box and their pallid faces. Her horrified scream brought the rest of the company running in a tumult. They, too, stopped dead when they saw what the others were looking at. The silence was broken by Maddy, who, in tears of rage, flung on to the floor the little celluloid doll dressed as Lucky and jumped on it again and again, hysterical with anger. The need to calm her brought them to their senses again, and Sandra put her arms round her little sister and told her not to be a silly girl.

'We'll get it back,' she told her. The police will catch him.'

'It's not—it's not that...' sobbed Maddy, distressed by her first contact with the falseness of human beings. 'It's because he *did* it... And we thought he was all right—I liked him... I didn't at first, but then...' She had to stop to gasp for breath.

Nigel reached for the telephone and said to the operator, 'Will you give me the police station, please. It's rather urgent.'

As he gave details to the friendly but unmoved police sergeant at the other end, the rest of the Blue Doors, pale and frightened, talked in little groups, softly, stunned, yet occasionally flaring into sudden spurts of rage.

Nigel, who suddenly looked very old, said, 'You'd all better go home. The parents will be worried. Don't tell them about this until we're really positive he has taken it. I must stay here to interview the police.'

They put on their coats and went out into the unfriendly cold and darkness. Maddy whimpered all the way home, and the boys made the night ugly with threats of what they would do to Lucky when he was caught.

55

'It's the low cunning of it that revolts me,' said Lyn. 'Worming his way into the job and into our affections! No wonder he worked so jolly hard—we wondered why. It was all for himself he was trying to rake in the money—we ought to have guessed. He obviously wasn't the type to be trusted. We all felt it at first. Why didn't we stick to it?'

'Because he seemed so—so...' Vicky searched for words, 'friendly and enthusiastic.'

'Friendly!' growled Bulldog. 'Gosh I'll let him know what I think of that type of friendship—'

'I feel awful—us going now,' said Snooks; 'leaving you when things are so bad—'

Sandra said sensibly, 'They're not as bad as all that. We mustn't let ourselves be dramatic about this. Of course he'll be caught and dealt with and our money recovered. This isn't the first time that this sort of thing has happened. It's happened to other people, but never to us, so naturally it's a shock.'

'Oh, stop being so self-controlled for goodness sake,' cried Lyn. 'You drive me mad with your good sense.'

'I'm sorry,' said Sandra, 'but it strikes me as better than losing our heads.'

Jeremy quelled them, 'Be quiet, you two. This is no time to bicker. We must stick together now, if ever we do.'

For many hours that night Nigel was with the police. They examined the box-office and the cash-box, took some finger prints from it and made Nigel go down to the station and make a statement. When he crawled into bed in the not-so-early hours of the morning he felt that he was the most wretched and ill-fated actor-manager in England.

The next day the police were still about the theatre, assuring them constantly that they would soon track down Mr Lucky. They also told the Blue Doors that he had a police record, and this was not the first time that he had absconded with the takings of some small theatre.

'The beast,' Vicky muttered, 'picking on people who are struggling to make a living...'

When their parents heard how they had been let down, they were full of sympathy, and promised any help they could give in tracking down Lucky. The six fairies departed sadly after extracting promises from the Blue Doors to let them know if there were ever anything they could do to help.

On Monday they hardly had the heart to rehearse *Granite*, but felt they must, as time was getting short. Nigel had to keep dashing away to answer calls from the police on the telephone, and to interview reporters.

'At least it's good publicity,' he said grimly. 'The sort that Lucky would approve of.'

'You don't think—' began Maddy hopefully.

'No,' said Nigel, 'I don't think that it's just a stunt. I'm positive it's the real thing. It *explains* Lucky. We never could quite place him, could we?'

'We know where he should be placed now,' said Jeremy bitterly, and then to Nigel, 'Nigel, what are we going to do now? Can we carry on?'

Nigel said with tight-set lips, 'I don't know. Mr Chubb is getting up tomorrow, and he'll be down at the theatre to go over the accounts with me. Then we shall know.'

Next day Mr Chubb appeared, very pale and much thinner from his illness, and extremely worried about the situation as there was no word from the police. His first words to Nigel were, 'If only we'd been insured—'

'"If only's" are no good,' said Nigel. 'There are endless ones—if only you'd never been ill—if only we'd never trusted Lucky. What we've got to do is to get down to it, and work out if we can possibly carry on.' They went into conclave in the box-office, poring over the accounts, wincing every time they realized how well in hand they would have been, were it not for Lucky.

The others were nervously rehearsing without Nigel, but every now and then someone would dry up completely and say, 'I'm sorry, but it's so difficult to concentrate.' Finally they gave it up and went over to the café for a cup of tea, and sat looking at the dirty table-cloth with unseeing eyes. Across the road, the little theatre, smartly painted in blue and cream, seemed as if it had never before meant so much to them.

Vicky broke the silence. 'And to think,' she said, 'that he is somewhere—walking about—eating and sleeping—'

'And all on our money,' added Bulldog. 'I bet he's killing himself at the thought of us. "Mugs"—that's the word he'd use to describe us.'

'And it's so right,' said Lyn.

''Ave you 'eard anything?' inquired the friendly waitress who adored them all.

'Not yet,' Jeremy said wearily. 'At first the police said they'd trace him easily, but it seems to be taking longer than they thought.'

'Oh, I'm that sorry—and just when you was doin' so nicely...' In her distress for them she slopped the tea into the saucers of the cups she was carrying, and sniffed loudly.

They sat in silence. The thaw had set in, and outside the grimy windows the snow drip-dripped off the roofs on to the wet pavements. They kept a constant watch on the front entrance of the theatre, waiting for Nigel and Mr Chubb to appear. When at last they did, there was nothing to be gathered from their faces. They would have looked as pale as that anyhow. But when they had joined them at the table and ordered tea, Nigel looked up and said in a dead voice, 'Well, we've been over the accounts, and you are all welcome to do the same to make sure that you agree with us, that the only possible thing that we can do in the circumstances...' He swallowed convulsively, 'is to close down.'

6

THE UNEMPLOYED

Lyn woke up and was just about to leap out of bed in order to get to rehearsal in time, when she remembered that there was no rehearsal. There was no show. There was no company. There was no Blue Door Theatre. The horror of it dawning on her again, after the respite of sleep, dissolved her into tears, and she buried her face in the pillow which was still damp from last night's weeping. After a while a sudden hope struck her. Perhaps there was some news from the police that Lucky had been caught. She threw on her dressing-gown and hurried downstairs. Jeremy was on the telephone.

'Any news?' she gasped.

'I see. Thank you,' he said into the receiver, and then hung up.

'No,' he told her despondently. 'The police say there is nothing to report, and please will we not make continual inquiries. They will get in touch with us when there is any news.'

'We're not even allowed to inquire,' cried Lyn. 'That at least was something to do...'

'Something to do' was becoming a very important item in their lives, after a week with no show to rehearse. Straight from the rush and flurry of repertory, the sudden inactivity seemed uncanny.

'What on earth shall we do today?' demanded Jeremy.

'Have breakfast, go out and have coffee, and answer a lot of stupid inquiries from stupid people about the theatre. Have lunch. Can't afford to go to the pictures. Have tea. Have supper, then go to bed,' said Lyn gloomily.

Jeremy paced up and down the hall. 'We can't go on like this. We shall go crazy.'

'Yet we can't go anywhere,' said Lyn. 'We must be here on the spot to start again immediately, if they should get the money back.'

Jeremy said slowly, 'Do you really still believe that they'll get the money back?'

Lyn considered it, and then said, 'No, I don't think they will. But if there were not that to hope for, there would be nothing—'

'Breakfast!' cried Mrs Darwin cheerily. Over their toast and marmalade Mrs Darwin said, 'Oh, Lyn, I've got so much shopping for you to do this morning... And Jeremy, your father said something about you dropping in to the office and helping him out with a job or two.' They agreed unenthusiastically. The parents of all the Blue Doors were making a gallant effort to keep them busy, but nothing could ever make them busy enough to take their minds off the loss of the theatre.

That morning at eleven o'clock it was a despondent and depleted company who assembled at Bonner's for their mid-morning coffee. The six fairies had departed. Terry had returned to Tutworth Wells to the company that he had been with before, until he might be needed by the Blue Doors again. Ali and Billy had gone back to London to see their parents, and, as they sat down at the large table in the window that they usually occupied, Myrtle said nervously, 'Oh, Nigel, I don't want you to think I am backing out, or anything...' Her heavy friendly face was lined with distress; 'but I've been offered another rep. job, quite near here...' She named the nearest town to Fenchester that had a theatre; 'and I'd be able to keep in touch...'

'Why, yes, of course you must take it,' said Nigel hastily. 'I can't keep you hanging about here in the hope that we may be able to start up again. Of course you must go.'

'I go back to the Academy tomorrow,' mourned Maddy, 'and I pity anyone who asks me if I've had good holidays.'

The six remaining Blue Doors looked from one to the other with the horrible feeling of being aboard a sinking ship. And then a too familiar voice cut into the silence.

'Ah, dear kiddies...' They looked up—into the puffy, but somewhat paler, features of Mrs Potter-Smith. 'Congratulate me, dears,' she cried. 'This is my first public appearance since my illness. Pneumonia, you know. That draughty theatre of yours was to blame, I'm afraid. But there—Art for Art's sake, as I always say. Though I must say I didn't care much for the little play you were doing. But what's the news I hear now? You've closed down? Couldn't make it pay? Oh, dear me! How sad.'

'It was just beginning to pay very well indeed,' said Nigel loudly. 'We were recovering from the harm that your pneumonia did to us, and we were robbed by the box-office manager—'

'Not that nice Mr Chubb?'

'No. He, too, has been ill. This was—someone else—'

'Rather convenient, in a way. I suppose,' said Mrs Potter-Smith, nodding her head understandingly, so that the feathers in her hat shook; 'I mean, it gives you an excuse to close down, doesn't it, and no-one will expect you to pay back the loan to the Town Council.'

Waves of hatred seemed to fill the air round the heads of the Blue Doors. Then Maddy said airily, 'Oh, we're paying that back all right. I've got a lot of money put away from that film I did. Do you remember? You were an extra in it.'

Mrs Potter-Smith seemed a little put out, and said, 'Oh, really? It seems a pity to have to dig into poor little Maddy's savings to get you older ones out of a jam, doesn't it? Well, I must fly. I'm meeting one of my pals, Miss Thropple, you know. We have a chin-wag here every Tuesday.' And off she sailed.

'Chin-wag is the word,' remarked Bulldog venomously. 'All six of them.'

Maddy said earnestly, 'Nigel, I meant what I said just now. Do let's pay the Town Council with my film money. Then no-one can say that Lucky robbing us was a fake."

'No,' said Nigel firmly. 'We're paying back that money from Blue Doors funds, and not from any other source.'

Maddy sighed. 'Everyone seems determined to stop me spending that money. What's the good of having it—just sitting in the bank like that?'

'We can't let you, Maddy dear,' said Sandra, 'even if it's only to stop Mrs Potter-Smith and her cronies saying things like she said just now.'

'I thought people hardly ever got over pneumonia,' said Maddy in a disappointed voice.

'Mrs Potter-Smith is immortal,' observed Jeremy, staring miserably into his coffee.

'What shall we do this afternoon?' demanded Vicky.

'Something that doesn't need any money,' said Bulldog.

'Yes, isn't it terrible,' agreed Sandra. 'I haven't got a sou—and I just *can't* ask Mummy and Daddy for any. I'm out of the habit of getting pocket-money every week.'

'My mother tactfully never asks for the change from the shopping,' said Lyn bitterly. 'It's sweet of her, but it makes me feel like the poor relation.'

'Come on. We'd better go,' said Bulldog. 'We've been here an hour and a half, and that's quite long enough for one cup of coffee each.'

'By next week we shall be asking for one cup amongst us and six straws.'

'Nigel,' said Sandra, as they walked down the High Street, 'you don't think there's any chance of our opening up again within the next few weeks, do you?'

'I haven't an idea. But even if the police got the money back, we couldn't open up for a couple of weeks. Why?'

'Well, I bumped into my old cookery teacher yesterday, and she said if I wanted something to do to pass the time I could go and help her give cookery demonstrations at evening classes.'

'Oh, Sandra,' exclaimed Lyn. 'You can't!'

'Why can't I? It'll be something to do. And it will give me some pocket-money.'

'But—but everyone in Fenchester knows you as an actress.'

'But actresses also eat,' observed Sandra.

'That's rather good,' said Jeremy, trying it out. 'Actors also eat. That will have to be our motto for a while, I think.'

'But what gets me down,' blazed Lyn, 'is that we've got to knuckle under, and do what everyone always advised us to do—get sensible and dependable jobs just so that we shall be safe.'

'You don't have to,' said Nigel. 'You could go back to London and try your luck again.'

'On what?' demanded Lyn. 'I haven't got a penny to my name. And I must be here, in case we get the money back suddenly and start again.'

They trailed wretchedly along, with the cold wind blowing against them, occasionally having to acknowledge acquaintances who looked at them curiously, pityingly.

'Let's—let's go down to the theatre this afternoon,' said Maddy suddenly.

'No,' cried Lyn. 'I couldn't bear it.'

'Well, I must,' said Maddy, 'to collect my grease-paint and things to take back to the Academy.'

'Yes,' said Nigel, 'it might be as well to take a few belongings out of the dressing-rooms. The Council may want to let it.'

As they collected up their belongings that afternoon they spoke in lowered tones, and it seemed as though the theatre had been empty for a long time. Just as they were about to leave it, Lyn suddenly put down her suitcase and said loudly and firmly, 'No!' They all turned and looked at her.

'I will not leave this theatre until we have decided what our plan of campaign is to be. As it is we're just sitting back and—and knuckling under. We can't just leave our careers hanging in mid-air like this, and slouch around Fenchester until our parents find ghastly dull jobs for us. Now! What shall we do?'

Slowly the old flame of ambition was kindled in the hearts of the Blue Doors. They looked around their theatre, seeking for inspiration. Then Bulldog said, 'But it's obvious—'

'What?' they cried.

'Find Lucky.' His large face beamed with enlightenment. 'That's it, isn't it? He's got our money, and the police can't find him—so we must.'

Nigel whistled thoughtfully. 'How would we go about it?'

'A little amateur detective work,' said Bulldog. 'We've read about it often enough in books. So we should know how to set about it.'

'I suppose you fancy yourself as Bulldog Drummond.'

'Be sensible, Maddy. This is serious,' Jeremy reprimanded her.

'Yes,' said Nigel. 'Lucky must be somewhere. And we've got a more personal interest in finding him than the police have—'

'But what about the parents?' Maddy wanted to know, adding sagely, 'they'd call it a wild goose chase.'

'Yes, I'm afraid they wouldn't have to know,' said Jeremy, 'but we must remember that we haven't any money.'

'Oh, gosh,' said Vicky. 'It always comes back to the same thing.'

Mechanically they had grouped themselves round the stove, although it was not alight. Sandra held out her hands to the imaginary warmth, and said thoughtfully, 'I've got an idea—'

'Cough it up,' said Maddy vulgarly.

'Why don't we split up? The boys to chase Lucky—because it's more of a man's job, and we three girls to finance the search. We could just disappear, and go round trying to get work—preferably theatre work because it pays better—but taking anything that will make money, and sending as much as we can to the boys so that they can continue—'

'But what about me?' wailed Maddy. 'I suppose I'll be stuck in the Academy like a pig in a poke.'

'The simile is yours,' smiled Nigel, already elated by the new plan. 'No, Maddy. You could be very useful at the Academy. You would be our headquarters. We would use you as a permanent address, and communicate through you.'

'I'll direct proceedings,' shouted Maddy excitedly. 'Calling all Blue Doors—calling all Blue Doors...' she parodied. 'Proceed at once to Piccadilly Circus, where Lucky is resisting arrest.'

Bulldog's eyes were shining. 'It would be fun. It would be exciting. It would be something to do. We shouldn't just be sitting waiting.' His face clouded suddenly. 'But fancy being supported by a lot of girls...' They laughed at his crestfallen expression. It was the first time that laughter had rung through the theatre for many days.

'Yes, yes,' said Vicky, 'it would be a fine idea. We'd be supporting you, but on the other hand, we'd be going on with our acting—*if* we can get jobs.'

'Rep., I should think,' said Sandra. 'Because it's cheaper living in the provinces than in London. We could live in working girls' hostels.'

Ideas were tumbling out of them now.

'We must just disappear—all of us—at once, before we're shoved into the local Ministry of Nincompoops as office boys.'

'What shall we do for money to get started?'

'Sell something. What?'

'Our clothes—'

'Yes, that's right. We've all got large wardrobes now, having done a long rep. season. And we shall only have to have necessities with us—'

'One change of clothing,' added Bulldog.

'It'll be better than helping out at cookery classes, won't it, Sandra?'

'It will,' said Sandra carefully, 'if it's a success... if you boys find him... if we can manage to keep you going... if we can get enough work. Travelling expenses will be the difficulty.'

'Stooge!' cried Maddy. 'Hitch-hike.'

'Of course,' said Nigel 'We shan't have money to spare for things like trains.'

'But what happens,' said Sandra, 'if we don't find him?'

'Stop "iffing" for goodness sake!' cried Lyn. 'Don't you see that now we're alive again? We're starting to *do* something! There's no time for "ifs".'

'What is the first thing to do?' demanded Vicky.

'Sell our clothes,' said Nigel.

'The difficulty will be getting them out of the house without our parents asking a lot of difficult questions.'

'Nonsense,' said Lyn. 'We've come out with cases today, collecting things from the theatre, so why shouldn't we tomorrow? No-one will know whether they're full or empty—'

'Exactly,' said Nigel. 'But another important thing is to get a clue as to where we are to start looking for Lucky.'

'London,' said Vicky promptly.

'Why?'

'He had a Cockney accent.'

'Yes,' agreed Nigel. 'But that isn't necessarily where he has gone. I think the first thing to do tomorrow after selling the clothes is to visit his landlady, and see if she can help us.'

'The police have questioned her a lot,' objected Bulldog.

'But she's probably frightened of the police. We must just chat, not question her. In fact, we'll pay the rent he owed when he left. That'll help.'

'With the proceeds from my new dinner-jacket, most probably,' mourned Bulldog.

'Well, you always did look rather a funny shape in it,' Maddy comforted him. 'Going out where you should go in.' The scuffle that followed was quite like old times, and they resumed the discussion breathless but enthusiastic. They were, in fact, quite hilarious at the prospect of a new adventure, of doing something definite.

'It'll be grand,' said Vicky romantically. 'We shall be out on the open road—seeking our fortunes—or rather not *our* fortunes, but our theatre's fortune.'

'And *we* shall be mysterious sleuths, dodging like shadows in pursuit of the culprit.'

Nigel and Sandra shook their heads in a pitying fashion at these highly coloured word-pictures.

'And I shall be the brains behind it all,' Maddy chimed in, 'sitting in my den in the Academy, smoking a Meerschaumer—or whatever it is—and saying "Elementary, my dear Buster" at intervals.'

'What,' said Sandra 'about our parents?' Their merriment faded, and they shuffled uneasily.

'Of course, they'll be upset, our disappearing like that, but it's no good telling them—'

'We must leave them notes,' said Sandra; 'you boys telling them that you've gone to London to look for work and keep a look out for Lucky, and we'll say we're going round the reps. for work. That's quite true. And we'll explain that we didn't tell them beforehand, in case they dissuaded us from going.'

'And when the money is found,' said Maddy, 'they'll be terribly glad, because they'll have us home again.' But they still felt a little guilty at planning to deceive their parents.

'After all, we're not kids any more,' said Nigel, after a pause, 'except Maddy, and she'll be safely at the Academy.' Sandra frowned at him. 'Being the brains of it all,' he added hastily.

'Well, is everything settled?' demanded Lyn. 'We sell clothes tomorrow?'

'Oh, and I've got some jewellery,' added Vicky. 'It was left to me by our grandmother.'

'Good. That can go too. And we can see Lucky's landlady so that you boys can pick up the scent. O.K.?'

'We must succeed,' said Lyn passionately. She stalked round the auditorium just as she used to when she was much younger, and was impressing on the others how bent she was on becoming an actress. Her face and body were taut with determination as she looked around, seeming to challenge the very walls of the place.

'I will not sit around accepting things as they come,' she cried. 'I will not be a failure.'

7

SPLIT UP

The second-hand clothes shop smelt very strange. It was a mixture of moth balls, old boots and the gas from the gas fire that blared and hissed in the corner. Mrs Mintey, the proprietress, was enormous, and seemed to be wearing all the most outlandish specimens from her stock. Her dress was trimmed with black jet, and over it she wore a mauve woolly cardigan. On her head was a man's check cloth cap, and her wrists jangled with bracelets—charm bracelets, gold bracelets, ivory bracelets—all her most valuable pieces were there.

The Blue Doors had spent a distressing morning tramping round the second-hand dealers with their bulging suitcases. Selling their clothes had not turned out to be as easy as they had expected. The better-class dealers sold only on commission, which would have meant waiting until the garments were re-sold before collecting their money. One very superior proprietress had opened Lyn's case, and, fingering a little black dress to which

71

she had been devoted, said, 'Rather worn, isn't it? And we really only buy up models.' Lyn had been so offended that they had all turned round and walked out of the shop.

And now Mrs Mintey was turning over their clothes with fat dirty fingers like sausages. She finished off Vicky's and said firmly, 'Six pounds.' Then she started on Sandra's, muttering under her breath the value of each garment. Sandra could hardly bear to watch. There went the lovely dress she had made herself for Cinderella's ball dress, in their amateur days...

'Six bob,' said Mrs Mintey, hissing through her broken teeth. And now her ballet skirt from the Academy...

'Five bob,' was the verdict on it. And there was the evening dress that she had worn on the fatal night when they had discovered Lucky's disappearance. She had only worn it twice... Vicky put her arm through Sandra's.

'Think how lovely it will be each morning, not to have to wonder what to put on.' They had allowed themselves only slacks, jersey, heavy coat, scarf and boots, and the girls also had tweed skirts, so that they could look ladylike if need be.

'How we're going to manage if we get into rep. I can't imagine,' sighed Sandra.

'We'll just have to borrow,' said Vicky. 'Thank goodness rep. people are good about lending.'

'Seven quid,' said Mrs Mintey stolidly, closing Sandra's case. 'And that's bein' generous, mind.'

'I'm sure it is,' said Sandra sadly, as she took the grubby notes that were offered her.

When they got out of the shop, Nigel said, 'Congratulations, girls.'

'Why?'

'I knew you'd sacrifice a lot for the Blue Door Theatre, but I never thought I'd see you selling up your wardrobes without turning a hair.'

'Several of my hairs turned,' admitted Sandra. 'But it's necessary, so it can't be helped.'

'And what,' said Bulldog, 'is the next step?'

'Go home and dump our suitcases,' said Nigel, 'and then call on Lucky's landlandy.'

'I don't think all of us had better go,' observed Jeremy. 'We might frighten her. Nigel, you'd better go.'

'And one of the girls,' said Nigel.

'Sandra,' said Lyn. 'She's the most tactful, and can make polite conversation.'

As they made their way home a taxi stopped by them, and Maddy, on her way to the station, popped her head out.

'I'm in a frightful hurry. Can't stop. How did you get on? Much money? Must go... Good luck. Keep in touch. Hound him down, won't you?' she gabbled. Then, to the driver, 'The station, quickly—and don't spare the horsepower,' and the taxi shot off before they had time to say a word.

'Yes, it will be useful having Maddy at the Academy,' said Nigel thoughtfully. 'She can keep us in touch with each other.'

Nigel and Sandra got rid of their cases, and then went round to Lucky's landlady's house, which was not far away from their homes. They knocked on Mrs Quantock's door, and when she opened it she did not look at all pleased to see them.

'Oh, no,' she quavered, before they had time to speak.

'I can't take in any more theatricals—not after the last—not after Mr Lucky. Lucky, indeed—Unlucky, I'd call him. Left owing me three pounds, 'e did. I know 'e robbed you left and right, o' course—but still—three pounds—'

'But, Mrs Quantock,' cut in Nigel smoothly, 'we haven't come to ask you to take in any more lodgers. We've come to pay you back your money.'

Her grey face brightened immediately. 'Oh, Mr Nigel—you shouldn't reelly!' But her hand was already out-stretched for the notes that Nigel had produced with a flourish from his wallet. He gave her three from the five which he had raised on a very nice lounge suit, a silk dressing-gown and two sports coats.

'How is your rheumatism, Mrs Quantock?' asked Sandra kindly. She wasn't sure that Mrs Quantock *had* rheumatism, but it seemed a pretty safe bet.

'Chronic, miss, in this cold weather,' said Mrs Quantock.

'Won't you come in and have a bit of warm?' She did not have to ask them twice. When they were sitting round the range in her kitchen, she said, 'Oh, yes, it's a bad business about Mr Lucky. They 'aven't found 'im yet, I suppose?'

'Not yet,' said Nigel, 'but I expect they will. The police have been working on it. I expect they bothered you with a lot of questions?'

'Oh, yes, but I couldn't 'elp them. 'E used to talk a lot, but never said much, if you know what I mean. I knew he lived in London somewhere, and 'ad worked at a lot of different things, but that's all.'

'I suppose he didn't leave any belongings behind?'

'Nothing much. The police took all the bits and pieces 'e did leave.' Sandra and Nigel exchanged a despairing glance. ''Ow about a cupper tea? The kettle's on the boil.'

74

'That would be very nice,' said Sandra, and Mrs Quantock hurried off into the scullery. While she was gone, Nigel wandered disconsolately round the room, peering into corners.

'It seems so easy in a film. Clues seem to sprout from everywhere—gosh!'

'What?' said Sandra jumping. Nigel was squatting in a corner grovelling in the waste paper basket. He held up some fragments of paper.

'Here's something the police didn't get. This can't have been emptied for ages. Look...' It was an envelope torn in half, with an address on the front that read 'Mr L. Green, The Blue Dore Theatre, Fenchester, Fenshire,' and on the back of the letter in large ungainly handwriting, 'From Mrs Green, 5, Linden Grove, S.E.'

'His wife—his mother...' conjectured Sandra.

'We shall see,' said Nigel, softly and determinedly, as Mrs Quantock returned with the tea. They could hardly contain themselves as they supped it.

Sandra said casually, 'Was Mr Lucky married, do you know?'

''E never mentioned it as I remember,' said Mrs Quantock, gulping her tea appreciatively. ''E did mention 'is mother once— "the old girl", 'e called 'er. But 'e seemed quite fond of her, I thought.'

'Well, we must be getting along,' said Nigel as they finished their tea.

As soon as the front door was closed behind them, Nigel produced the envelope again, and they studied it eagerly.

'The letter wasn't in the basket too?' inquired Sandra.

'No, I don't think so. But this is something to go on—a great help. If we can see his mother we may get something out of her.

She obviously corresponds with him.' They raced back to tell the other Blue Doors.

'A clue—a clue—' cried Bulldog, swinging ecstatically on the garden gate.

'Sh!' they all turned on him, and glanced uneasily at the windows of their houses. The problem of getting away unobserved was now uppermost in their minds.

'It must be tonight,' said Lyn, 'while we're still enthusiastic over the clue.'

'It'll be easy,' said Bulldog. 'Don't you remember how we did it once before, to go tobogganing?'

'This is rather different, isn't it?' said Nigel. They heaved sighs and thought how young they had been in those days before they went to the Academy. They lingered at their gates, unwilling to go in for the evening meal, because it would mean the last lap—after that there would only be bedtime—and the setting off on this most uncertain of adventures.

At dinner Jeremy's father said, 'Well, old man, what do you say to coming into the business? You'd have to start at the bottom, you know, and work upwards, but it'd be a good job when you got to the top—and—well, you know I've always hoped that's what would happen. I'd pay you a wage at first, even though you'd only be learning.'

Jeremy blushed and stammered and caught Lyn's eye, who said, 'Well, Jerry?'

'I'll think it over, if I may.' Mr Darwin appeared pleased and attacked his dinner in good humour, still talking of the business and how useful it would be to have Jeremy in it too. Jeremy writhed, and grew more and more uncomfortable, while the worse state he got himself into the more contained Lynette became.

'Yes, Daddy,' she heard herself saying, 'it will be nice for you to have someone in the family connected with the business...' Jeremy was amazed at the duplicity of his sister.

'Well, Jeremy,' said Mr Darwin, at the end of the meal, 'drop into the office tomorrow for a start, if you're around.'

'If I'm around,' repeated Jeremy, feeling hot and cold all over. When the parents had left the room, he exclaimed, 'Lyn! How could you go on like that—'

'Well, you were gibbering like a baboon. Someone had to say something!'

'But all that—building up his hopes like that—'

'I'm sorry,' said Lyn. 'I suppose it *was* mean, but I got carried away by my part. After all, I am an actress. And it's all for the sake of the theatre, isn't it?'

'You're a conscienceless creature,' observed Jeremy, 'in some things. I felt ghastly.'

In the Fayne household things were no better. Sandra and her mother sat sewing by the fire.

'How quiet it seems without Maddy,' observed Mrs Fayne.

'Doesn't it?' agreed Sandra.

'I'm so glad you're still with me. It was even worse when you were all away.' Sandra could not trust herself to speak.

'And it's nice that you're going to do the cookery classes. That will be something to keep you occupied, but not a full-time job. I don't think you need to look for anything else to do. You're really very valuable to me about the house.'

'Oh, Mummy—' Sandra nearly came out with the whole thing, but she was interrupted.

'Oh, darling, how tactless of me! I know you're upset about the theatre. And we do feel for you. And we'll do anything we can to help you, you know that. You've been awfully brave about it really.'

Sandra dropped her sewing and flung her arms round her mother's neck. 'You are sweet,' she said, 'Goodnight,' and she ran upstairs to bed feeling like a traitor.

When the Halfords trooped in to say goodnight to their mother they found her sitting up in a pretty pink dressing-jacket, looking better than usual. They sat on her bed and she asked what they had been doing all day. This was rather difficult to answer, but before they could do so, she produced a bottle of mulberry wine.

'Look, dears, the doctor has ordered me this—thinks it'll do me good. But it's probably ghastly. Do help me out...'

They sipped the sweet red liquid from tooth-mugs, which were all that was available, and there was a pleasant midnight feastish atmosphere, if only their hearts had not been so heavy with guilt.

'Darling,' she said to Vicky, 'I think you ought to start your dancing lessons again. You'll get terribly out of practice, you know.'

'Can't afford it,' Vicky mumbled.

'Don't be silly, dear. Daddy can manage it. I'm sure he'd let you.' Vicky traced patterns on the counterpane.

Mrs Halford sighed. 'Oh, I wish I had the chance.' It was rarely that she referred to the accident which had cut short her career as a dancer.

Vicky said quickly, 'Oh, Mummy, I'm not being ungrateful! I'd love to—but—'

At this moment their father came in, saying, 'Bedtime, you gang. Mother's had enough of you for one evening, I'm sure.'

As they went to their rooms Bulldog muttered, 'If only they wouldn't be so *nice* to us—'

Vicky stopped dead on the landing. 'Oh, why ever are we behaving in this kiddish fashion? Why don't we go straight back and *tell* them what we are going to do. Then they wouldn't be hurt.'

'Vicky!' expostulated Nigel. 'We can't. You know there'd be a lot of fuss and bother and "Why not wait till the morning?" And you know that if we don't start now, we never will.'

'Yes,' sighed Vicky. 'You're right. I was just feeling homesick in advance, if you know what I mean.' Nigel did.

As the clock struck twelve there were creakings on the stairs of the three houses, and six shadowy figures emerged from their front doors, carrying the smallest cases and grips that would contain a toothbrush and one change of clothing. They had banned haversacks, as they felt that these might attract too much attention. Cases were more anonymous.

It was very cold. The wind whistled down the avenue, blowing the little trees about under a moon that was constantly obscured by hurrying clouds. For a few seconds they stood in a silent group, and looked up at their homes, then Nigel said, 'Come on,' and they turned away and trudged off in the direction that led out of the town towards London. When they had gone a few yards, Nigel said, 'Where are you girls making for?'

'We're going as far west as we can. Penzance or thereabouts. And then coming slowly back, calling at all the theatres and trying to get work for as long as possible in each of them. If one of us gets work in any town for a bit, the other two will take any old job in the same town until the one that's working is ready to move on. Do you think that's O.K.?'

'Fine,' said Nigel. 'Do look after yourselves, won't you?'

'Of course. And the same to you. Your mission is more dangerous than ours.'

The town was strangely deserted. They did not meet a soul along the windy streets. As they left the town a policeman shone his torch on them suspiciously.

'Don't you glare at us like that,' murmured Jeremy. 'We're going off to do your job for you...'

'Do you think we shall walk all night?' asked Vicky rather tremulously as they passed Fennymead.

'No,' said Bulldog, 'there's loads of night transport.'

They strained their ears for the sound of traffic, but only heard the singing of the telegraph wires.

'We are fools,' said Sandra. 'We could be safely in our warm little beds—'

'Regretting it already?' demanded Nigel.

'No, I'm not. But I still think we're fools.'

They trudged in silence for a while, each occupied with rather sober thoughts, then Jeremy said, 'Really, we don't want to go in the same direction, do we? You girls ought to turn off at the next cross roads.' The girls did not reply, but glanced uneasily round at the dark hedgerows.

'Perhaps we'll come a bit further with you and then turn off to the left, I mean the west,' said Vicky.

'Yes, good idea,' said Nigel quickly, feeling a little doubtful about leaving the three girls alone on the deserted roads in the middle of a cold winter's night.

'Listen! What's that?' cried Bulldog. They stood frozen like statues. Yes, faintly in the distance came the rumble of wheels. They shouted for joy.

'Perhaps it won't stop,' said Sandra.

'Oh, it must!' It was an enormous removal van that lurched and swayed as it swung round the bends. They signalled it frantically with an electric torch and it stopped with a grinding of brakes.

'London?' inquired the driver, sticking his head out of the window.

'Yes,' cried the boys. 'Three of us.'

'Not the three young ladies?'

'No,' said the three young ladies pathetically.

'I'll 'ave to put you in the back,' said the driver. 'Not supposed to carry passengers.' He nipped out, leaving the engine running, and let down the flap at the back of the lorry. Inside was a beautiful drawing-room suite—a couch and two chairs. The boys clambered up, and, shouting with laughter, arrayed themselves over the furniture. Bulldog lounged luxuriously back across the couch.

'Music-ho,' he shouted. 'Bring on the dancing girls.'

The girls waved and they all shouted 'Good luck' at the top of their voices, and then the flap was closed, and the racket the passengers were making was drowned by the roaring of the engine as the vehicle started off again.

'Chin up, girls,' shouted the driver, and stepped on the accelerator. For a long time they could hear the lorry fading into the distance of the silent night.

8

THE STREET CALLED LINDEN GROVE

As the lorry pulled up on the outskirts of London, Bulldog rolled off the sofa on to the floor with a bump. He sat up, rubbing his head and wondering wherever he was. Jeremy and Nigel, fast asleep in armchairs, stirred and groaned. The driver stuck his head through the dividing window.

'What part do you want?' he demanded. They looked at him with sleepy eyes, bewildered at waking up inside a lorry in upholstered chairs.

'What district?' he asked again.

'Oh, is this London?' asked Bulldog, staggering to his feet. 'This is where we get off.'

'We want the south-east side.'

'That's right,' said the driver. 'This'll do you 'ere then.'

They began to straighten themselves and to collect their pathetic pieces of luggage.

'Gosh, I'm stiff!' groaned Bulldog. 'And thirsty—'

'What I wouldn't give for a cup of tea—' agreed Jeremy.

'And bacon and eggs,' added Bulldog.

'We'll try and get some breakfast straight away,' said Nigel, 'to give us a chance to collect our wits a bit.'

The driver let down the flap and they clambered out. It was a cold day, still very early morning, and a light drizzle was falling.

'Cheerio!' shouted the driver, hopping back into his seat.

'Thanks a lot. Cheerio!' they shouted, feeling far from cheery. They were in a particularly depressing area, south of the river, where the buildings were grey and gaunt, the pavements were grey and wet, and the people who scrambled aboard the rocking trams were grey and anxious-looking.

'I feel like death,' grumbled Jeremy. 'I could do with a bath and shave.'

'That's out of the question,' said Nigel, 'but let's find some breakfast.' They trudged along the wet streets, and turned into the first café that was open. It had wooden tables between long wooden seats shaped like the church pews. A tired waitress served them with rather bad coffee and sausages and tomatoes that tasted good after the long journey. After a while they began to wake up a bit.

'Well,' said Bulldog, surreptitiously wiping his plate with a crust.

'Yes. What next?' said Jeremy.

'Make for number five Linden Grove, wherever that may be,' said Nigel, producing the envelope and studying it.

'It doesn't say where it is—just S.E. We'll have to ask a police-man.' Suddenly the funny side of this remark struck them, and they shouted with laughter, waking up a few tired night-shift workers who were dozing over their cups of tea before returning home to bed for the day.

'Imagine Sherlock Holmes asking a policeman the way,' guffawed Bulldog. They felt considerably better after a meal and a laugh, and when they left the café the sun was up and the rain had stopped.

They walked for a long way without seeing a policeman, and then, just as one came into sight, Jeremy said suddenly, 'I say—you don't think that our parents will be worried over our disappearing and get the police to look for us, do you?'

'No,' said Nigel. 'They wouldn't do that. Our notes will have looked after that. They'll know why we've gone, and see that it would be no good trying to get us back.' The policeman approached with a portly gait.

'Can you tell us the way to Linden Grove?' asked Nigel, rather nervously for all his assurances. After much head scratching and 'Ums' and 'Ahs' the policeman decided that the best way was to go to New Cross by bus, and then it was a tram-ride to Linden Grove. They thanked him and then started off.

'I wonder if we ought to try to walk to save fares?' suggested Jeremy.

'I don't think it would be worth it,' said Nigel. 'What we save in money we'd lose in time. And we must remember that time is jolly important. We've got to catch him before he spends all the money.'

They got on the bus and sat in silence until Nigel said anxiously, 'I hope the girls are all right. Let's ring Maddy up this afternoon and see if they have rung her.'

'I don't suppose they will have,' said Bulldog. 'It would be a trunk call, and they can't afford it.'

They each spent an uncomfortable few minutes thinking how awful it would be if they never heard from their sisters again. Then Nigel pulled himself together and said, 'Now look here, we must decide how we are going about this. What are we going to say when we get there?'

'Ask for Lucky,' said Bulldog promptly. Jeremy grinned.

'Supposing he came to the door—'

'My goodness,' threatened Bulldog, 'I'd—I'd...' He trailed off and said in a worried voice, 'What *would* we do?'

'Two of us hold him, while the other rings for the police,' said Nigel. 'Bulldog and I would hold him, and you could dash for the nearest phone-box, Jeremy, because you've got long legs.'

'You mean, of course,' said Jeremy, 'that I haven't got the strength to hold a flea, I know—'

'And that arrangement goes for any time we may find him,' continued Nigel.

'We'll ask to see him, and if he's not at home we'll ask where he is. We'll say we're friends of his.'

'We don't *look* like friends of his,' remarked Jeremy. They looked at each other as they got off the bus. They certainly did not look as flashy as any friends of Lucky's would look. Bulldog and Nigel had very shabby overcoats, and Jeremy wore his old navy-blue school macintosh which was by this time rather short in the sleeve and tight at the shoulder.

They were passing a men's cheap ready-made clothing shop, and with one accord they stopped and looked in the window. Displayed in many garish colours were some broad-brimmed hats like Lucky's. They looked at them longingly.

'Just the thing!' breathed Nigel.

'Quite cheap,' said Bulldog.

'And *hideous*,' added Jeremy. They looked at each other.

'Do you think we can afford them?' asked Nigel with a frown.

'They would be a help,' said Jeremy. Secretly, all three were longing to possess one.

'Yes,' said Nigel, and they dived into the shop.

The dapper little proprietor was quite hurt at the gusts of laughter with which his brand new line of hats was received.

'Oh, Bulldog!' groaned Nigel. 'What a thug you look!' Although the man kept reassuring them that they were 'all the go at the moment' they could not bring themselves to buy the more brightly coloured shades, but were satisfied with grey, brown and dark green. Handing over the money for their purchases they suddenly felt very guilty, thinking of the girls on the high road, imagining them weary and starving...

'I can't think *what* we're doing, buying hats at a time like this,' murmured Nigel. Then they strutted out on to the pavement, wearing the hats very self-consciously.

'Of course, with that macintosh, Jeremy, you look incredible,' remarked Nigel. 'For goodness sake take it off.'

'No, I'm cold,' objected Jeremy, then, 'oh, well, I'll take it off before we reach Lucky's.'

'I've had an idea,' said Bulldog.

'Did it hurt?' inquired Nigel sarcastically.

'Fooey to you. No, what I think is this. We ought to call at both the houses on either side of Lucky's as if we think that that's where he lives, and try to find out anything we can from them. They might know if he was home, whereas his mother, if she got suspicious, might pretend he wasn't.'

'A good idea,' said Nigel. 'Hey, this looks like the right tram.'

They took tickets to Linden Grove, and the tram swayed

and rattled and clanged over the lines. The boys began to feel nervous, wondering what lay in store for them—whether this would only prove to be the beginning or the end of their quest.

'Here we are!' shouted Nigel suddenly. 'There's the beginning of Linden Grove. Quick...' They leaped off the tram while it was still in motion, and Bulldog's beautiful green hat rolled into the wet road.

He picked it up and brushed it carefully with his cuff. Then, tilting it on his head at a jaunty angle, he said to the others in a passable imitation of Lucky's accent, 'Smashin', eh? Lead on, boss. I'm right behind yer.' And they struck off down the shabby street called Linden Grove.

The numbers decreased towards number five. At the end of the road they saw a black brick wall that formed part of a railway embankment. It was a depressing little street—not by any means a slum, and yet, somehow without hope. The trees that they had expected from the name were non-existent, and slatternly women peered out at them from behind grubby lace curtains.

'Fancy living here!' breathed Jeremy. 'I shouldn't think it would be any encouragement to an honest life.' They reached number five. It looked exactly the same as the two houses that joined it on either side.

'Let's go to number seven and number three first,' said Nigel in a whisper. They opened a rickety garden gate that led into a tiny patch of blackened earth where bits of old newspaper blew about, and knocked on the blistered front door. Their hearts were in their mouths. It seemed the first real step in their amateur detection. But there was no answer. The sound of the knocker died away, and there was no answering movement inside number three. It was a most unkind anticlimax.

'What a sell...' murmured Bulldog. Disconsolately they decided to try number seven. Here, a tousle-headed little girl with adenoids answered the door and gaped at them.

'Is your mother home, dear?' asked Nigel kindly.

'Ain't in,' said the child suspiciously.

'Well, is your father home?'

'Ain't.'

'Well, is *anyone* at home?'

'No, they ain't.' And she shut the door abruptly. They laughed ruefully.

'So much for your brilliant idea, Bulldog,' said Nigel. 'No, we'll have to go straight to the horse's mouth.'

In the patch of earth in front of number five someone had made gallant efforts to grow something, but what it was one could not discern from the tangle of brown and withered leaves. Now that the boys were actually here, it didn't seem such an important moment as they expected. They knocked, and immediately there were movements inside the house.

'I wonder—' Nigel just had time to breathe, and then the door was flung open. On the threshold stood an untidy little woman, smiling questioningly at them. She had Lucky's gay beady eyes and red cheeks. Her hair was escaping from a small bun on the back of her head, she wore a large apron splashed with soap-suds and she held her wet soapy hands out in front of her.

'Just doin' me smalls,' she cried cheerfully. 'Sorry, all.'

'Lucky in?' asked Nigel briskly, tipping his hat.

'Oh, no!' She expressed surprise at the question. 'Lucky's away on a job. Bin gone a long time. Down the country somewhere. I got 'is address. 'Ere, come in and I'll dry me 'ands and see if I can find it.' They crowded into the tiny passage, and she bustled off.

'On a job...' murmured Nigel. 'Do you think that means she *knows* what he does?' She came bustling back with a piece of paper in her hand. ''Ere we are.' She read out slowly, 'The—Blue—Door—The*ay*tre—Fenchester.' They could have screamed with disappointment.

Nigel broke in with, 'Oh, Mrs—er—Green, we—we saw Lucky at Fenchester. But he's not there any more.'

'No? Oh, well, I dunno then. 'E's a good boy, is Lucky, but not much of a one for letter writing. Mind, 'e writes when 'e can. Oh, 'e's a good boy in 'is way—'

'You don't know what sort of—job he's likely to be on now?'

'Same as the last, like as not. Theaytre business, you know. Pays well, 'e says. Oh, 'e's got 'is wits about 'im, 'as Lucky. But straight as a die, if you know what I mean. I always says to 'im when 'e was little, "Just you stick to the straight and narrer, me boy, never mind if you're not a millionaire."'

She laughed richly. 'But 'e 'asn't done too bad on the straight and narrer—you chaps in the same business?'

'Yes. More or less. And we've got a scheme we wanted to interest Lucky in. You haven't any idea when he might be coming back to town?'

'No—sorry. 'E might be 'ere now. 'E doesn't always stay at 'ome when 'e's in town, y'know. Sometimes 'e's in the West End, so as to be near 'is business.' She scratched her head thoughtfully. 'Now let me see... where might you find him? 'Course, 'e might walk in this door this very minute. You never know, with Lucky. 'Ere one minute—gorn the next—'

'You've said it,' agreed Bulldog. They had turned involuntarily to look at the door, but no Lucky appeared. Her brown eyes were alight with pride.

'Oh, that's the day, I tell you,' she continued, 'when 'e comes back. Pops up like a jack-in-the-box, grinning all over 'is face. "Ullo, old lady," 'e says—always calls me that—"'ere's yer bad penny turned up again."' She laughed happily, then added tenderly, 'And the presents 'e brings me—stockings—well, you never saw anything like them. Much too thin to wear, mind, but nice to keep by you fer weddings and funerals, like...'

The three boys were by now a bit embarrassed by this cascade of praise for the boy they were tracking down.

'And then 'e says, "Come on, old lady, you an' me are goin' out 'ittin the 'igh spots." An' out I 'ave to go, all dolled up, y'know. An' sometimes it's the dogs, or the music 'all or the pitchers; oh, we do 'ave a time...' Her face fell a bit. 'But I'd rather he stayed at 'ome a bit longer, than spent all that on me at once and then 'ave to go away on another job straight away.'

Nigel took advantage of the pause to say, 'Well if you really can't help us—' But Mrs Green was unwilling to lose her audience.

'No, wait a tick, and I'll 'ave another think... Might find 'im anywhere in the West End—goes to the races a lot, too. Let me think—'

'Where does he eat usually?' asked Jeremy suddenly. Her face lightened.

'Why, yes, of course. What am I thinking of! Nick's place, o' course.'

'Where?' they asked quickly, all together.

'Nick's Caff, it's called. I'm not sure where it is, but 'e talks about it quite a bit. In the West End, I think—or is it at the Elephant? No—up West, that's it.'

'But *where*?' asked Nigel agonized. She thought again.

'Oh, blowed if I know...' she said eventually. 'Take me up West and I'm lost, I tell you.'

They looked at each other hopelessly, then Nigel said, 'O.K., Mrs Green. We'll go and have a look for him.'

'That's right,' she nodded encouragingly. 'You hang round up West and you'll bump into him all right. If he's not in the country of course—and tell 'im 'is old lady'd like a look of him one of these days—'

'Yes, we'll tell him.' They made for the front door, which she opened for them.

'Well, I 'ope you find 'im. And if 'e comes 'ome, what names shall I say are lookin' for 'im?'

'Er—Jack—and Pete—and Joe,' said Nigel quickly, before the others had time to speak.

'Jack 'n' Pete 'n' Joe. Right you are. I'll tell 'im.' She waved with the corner of her apron and then closed the door.

They walked down the street in silence, then Nigel said heavily, 'Oh, gosh! I wish all this had never happened. She believes in him just like our mothers believe in us.'

'He's a better son to his mother than we are to ours,' observed Bulldog lugubriously. 'I'm sure we never make ours as happy as she is when he comes back.'

'But he's going to make her jolly unhappy before long,' Nigel reminded them. 'That's the worst of it. If he gets sent to prison it will break her heart!' For a moment their resolve weakened, then Nigel said, 'But we must think of the Blue Door Theatre.'

'And the girls.'

'And our parents. They'll want us home as much as Lucky's mother wants him—'

'Oh, let's stop drooling,' said Bulldog, pushing his hat to the back of his head. 'We've got to find Nick's Caff somewhere in the West End. That's a pretty tough proposition you know.'

'Not *so* tough,' said Nigel. 'Let's go into this phone-box and look through the directory.' The three of them crammed into the box and turned over the dog-eared pages.

'Nick's Autocars,' read Jeremy; 'Nick's Bar—Nick's Barber's Shop—bother—the rest of the page is torn out.'

'How maddening.' They walked about a mile to the next phone-box and read the rest of the page. But it was not much help to them. Nick's Hairdressing Salon and Nick's Music Stores—but no Nick's Caff. They looked at each other in despair, then left the phone-box.

'Here we come, Nick,' said Bulldog determinedly.

9

THE OPEN ROAD

The three girls plodded along the dark roads, talking busily to try to forget that they were alone between the hedges that curved dimly in front of them. They had begun planning the clothes they would buy when the money was found.

'And then I'd have a green velvet evening dress with a very low neck,' continued Vicky, then broke off abruptly as an eerie sound came from the field on their left.

'What's that?' she hissed in a terrified whisper. They stood very still, and Sandra peered through a gap in the hedge. Then she gave a hoot of laughter.

'It's only a cow, you idiot.' Vicky started off again, more quickly than before.

'Well, I'm not all that fond of cows...'

The heavier their cases became, the more exotic were their imaginary outfits. In the middle of describing a particularly luscious gold lamé house-coat, Sandra suddenly said, 'You know, if we're not careful we shall hardly be far out of Fenchester by daylight. That would be ridiculous.' Even as she was speaking, a faint buzz was heard in the distance.

'A car—a lorry—something, at any rate,' cried Sandra.

'Quick, Vicky, is the torch working?'

'Yes,' said Vicky, flicking it on and off.

They waited in a row by the roadside, and the headlights of a car grew gradually nearer. They signalled wildly, shouting 'Stop—Stop...' It was a large shiny car, and, as it drew up beside them they were horrified to see that on the front of it in large green letters was the word 'Taxi'.

'Oh, how mouldy!' sighed Vicky. The taxi-man did not seem at all surprised to see them.

'Where do you want?' he inquired. They did not quite know what to say.

'Er—we haven't really got much money...' explained Lyn embarrassed. 'You see, we're hitch-hiking.'

'How far are you going?'

'Well—quite a long way—'

'I'm going as far as Helmingthorpe. I'll give you a lift that far, if you like.' This was a small town about seven miles away. Thankfully they accepted the offer. It was warm and roomy inside and they curled up on the broad seat and were soon fast asleep.

'We'd need hats as well,' murmured Vicky, returning to the previous conversation, just before she dropped off into a heavy sleep.

They were wakened by a shaft of sunlight, and sat up, blinking. The taxi was standing in a small garage, and the sudden light had been caused by the opening of the doors. The taxi-man, grinning broadly, was walking towards them with three cups of tea on a tray. He opened the door with one hand, balancing the tray on the other.

'Your ladyships' tea,' he called out.

'Goodness!' gasped Sandra. 'Is it morning? I mean, have we been here all night?'

The taxi-man laughed. 'You have. When I put the old cab to bed last night you were sleeping like babes, so I didn't disturb you. And now you'd better come in and have a wash and brush up. The wife is cooking us a bit of breakfast.' He was a short plump man with thinning sandy-coloured hair and a friendly manner. The house was small but cosy, and the kitchen smelt deliciously of bacon and eggs as they made their way through it and up to the bathroom.

His wife seemed to take their presence for granted as much as he did, and provided them with soap and towels so that they did not need to unpack their tightly crammed little cases.

'I've never enjoyed a wash so much,' gasped Lyn, splashing cold water on her face.

Downstairs again in the kitchen they sat down to large plates of bacon and eggs, and demolished them speedily.

'Going on holiday?' asked their host.

'Er—sort of,' they answered.

'Bit early, aren't you?' demanded his wife. They laughed non-committally.

'Where are you making for?'

'Cornwall,' said Lyn.

'Hitch-hiking all the way?' the woman asked, raising her eyebrows.

'We hope so.'

'Well, it's one way to get about, Have you come far?'

'Not very,' said Lyn cautiously, and began to admire the flowers in the garden outside the window. Sandra was worrying about whether they should pay for the breakfast. It seemed insulting to offer to, and yet presuming on kindness not to. As they got up from the table, Lyn said firmly, 'Well, as we didn't pay for our ride last night, you must let us pay for our breakfast.'

'Get along with you,' cried the woman, horrified at the suggestion. 'The eggs are from our own chickens, and the ham from my brother-in-law's pig. What are you talking about?' The girls thanked their hosts profusely, and said that they must be on their way.

'I've got to do a job over the other side of Helmingthorpe at ten o' clock,' said the taxi-driver, 'so if you wait a bit, I'll take you when I go to collect my passenger. O.K.?'

They whiled away the time walking round the garden which was well stocked with flowers and vegetables, and watching the chickens squawking and fluttering in their runs. At five to ten they piled into the taxi again, and, shouting goodbyes to their benefactress, they were driven off.

'Well, if we're as lucky as this all the way, it won't be too bad,' remarked Sandra. They were quite sorry to leave their taxi-man, and his cab, but it was a brisk sunny morning and they strode off down the country road in fine style, taking deep breaths of the fresh air.

'This ought to do us a lot of good after the awful weather we've had, and being shut up indoors in the theatre all day,' said Sandra.

'But we mustn't forget our aim,' said Lyn. 'I'm afraid we're going to enjoy ourselves so much that we'll forget to look for work.'

'Oh, no, we shan't,' said Vicky, 'but let's get to the farthest point west where there is a theatre, and then we can really start.'

Their next lift was in a bread van which took them a few miles, with Lyn and Sandra squashed in the front beside the driver and Vicky in the back amongst the loaves. They smelt delicious and made her feel hungry, even though it was so soon after breakfast.

'I wonder how the boys are getting on,' mused Lyn.

'I wonder if our parents have found our notes yet,' said Sandra.

'I bet Maddy's wondering how we're getting on,' said Vicky.

''Ere, I say,' said the baker suddenly, 'you 'aven't run away from 'ome, 'ave yer?'

'Oh, no,' said Sandra. 'We're taking our holidays early this year.' But he looked at them suspiciously, and put them down at the next corner.

'Look here,' said Lyn, when they were alone again, 'we'd better get a story and stick to it. The truth is no good—it's too improbable. No-one would believe it.'

'I know what,' said Vicky. 'Let's take it in turn to explain what we're doing—then we can tell a different story each time. It'll give us something to think about.'

'But they must be possible stories,' said Sandra, 'and we mustn't giggle, otherwise it'll spoil it.'

'A good job Maddy isn't here. She'd tell the most amazing lies.' They were silent for a little while, walking along swinging their cases and thinking up reasons for their presence on the road at this time of year. The next car that came along was very smart—long and shiny and upholstered in dove grey. It was driven by an elderly lady in a smart hat and elaborate make-up.

She stopped when they pointed their thumbs in the direction she was going, and said, 'Er—yes?'

'Could you give us a lift?' Lyn asked politely. She looked at them questioningly. 'Have you missed the bus?'

'Yes,' said Sandra quickly.

'How far are you going?'

They hastily tried to think of the next town along the route but could not.

'Where are you making for?' asked Lyn.

'Castleford.'

'Oh, that would be lovely. If you don't mind...'

They clambered in, frightened of marking the smart upholstery that made their shabby coats and slacks look worse than ever.

'It's rather risky, isn't it?' inquired the lady, 'stopping cars on the road like this. I mean, you never know—'

'Oh, we thought you looked honest,' said Lyn nonchalantly. Sandra glared at her.

'I mean—well, it was very good of you to pick us up.'

'Are you sure you're all right?' the lady asked anxiously. 'I mean, you're not in need of help, or anything?'

'If only you knew how much we need some help...' thought Lyn, then said, 'Oh, no. It's quite all right, really. We're on our way to Penzance for a Girl Guides Rally. We wanted so much to go there, but we couldn't afford the fare.'

'Oh, what a shame!' cried the good lady. 'Well, I'll certainly take you as far as I can, but I haven't got much petrol, I'm afraid.'

'Oh, thank you very much,' they said, feeling rather guilty about their fabrications. She took them well beyond Castleford, and put them down with many good wishes for reaching the rally safely.

'That was a jolly good story,' said Vicky. 'I'm afraid all my ideas were much less possible than that.'

'But it sounds more possible than the truth does, doesn't it?' said Sandra. 'Imagine trying to explain the truth to anyone. It would sound like absolute fiction.'

'I say,' complained Lyn, 'I'm jolly thirsty. I wonder if we could get a glass of milk from this farm?' They walked through a yard where a large sheep dog barked a welcome at them, and the farmer's wife came to the door of the big stone-floored kitchen. For two-pence each they were soon drinking glasses of beautiful creamy milk with a froth on top. Much refreshed, they started off again, singing numbers from the pantomime at the tops of their voices. Several cars passed them by with a suspicious stare, but it was such a lovely day that they hardly minded. Then a neat little car driven by a woman of about thirty stopped and picked them up.

'How far are you going?' she inquired.

'As far as you can take us.'

'Well, I'm going a long way, almost into Devon.'

'Oh, how lovely,' cried Sandra. 'Can we come with you?'

'Of course. Jump in.' They flung themselves into the back, and she started off while they were still sorting out limbs and suitcases. She was neatly dressed in a tweed suit and felt hat, and there was something about her that made them think of a schoolmistress. 'And where are you girls off to?' she asked after a while. She had a very pleasant voice, rich and deep.

'Penzance,' said Sandra.

'And very nice too, especially at this time of year. It's so much pleasanter in Cornwall out of the tourist season. You're sensible to choose the very early spring like this, though it's a good job you didn't start off a few weeks earlier.'

They chatted about the bad weather they had suffered, and Sandra said without thinking, 'I'll never forget how cold I was during the week we did *Murder in Mid-Channel*.'

'Oh!' exclaimed the driver, 'of course. You're from The Blue Door Theatre at Fenchester, aren't you? I thought I'd seen you somewhere. I often stay at Helmingthorpe, and I go over to Fenchester just to go to the theatre. How are things?' There was a pause, and then it all came out in a rush—the bad weather, the success of the pantomime and Lucky's disappearance with the takings. She listened sympathetically, only inquiring, 'And what are you doing now?' They were shy of telling her—it seemed such a hare-brained scheme—but when they had explained, she nodded approvingly. 'It's certainly better than waiting for the police to get him. And I do hope you will be able to make ends meet while the search is on. I'm especially interested in your activities because I am a Drama Organizer for the West Country District.'

'Really?' said Lyn, with interest. 'What exactly does that mean?'

'Well, I'm in charge of the amateur drama in the schools and villages. I go round seeing their shows and giving advice, judging competitions sometimes, and rehearsing companies that are going into the finals of any important contests.'

'What an interesting job,' said Sandra. 'I'd have liked to do something like that, if I hadn't gone on the stage.'

'It's certainly very interesting,' said their new friend. 'But the only drawback, in my case, is that I have never been on the stage myself. I have taught elocution and have a degree in speech training, but that's not the same thing. I sometimes wish I had a bit of professional experience to fall back on. For instance, at the moment I've got several shows that are going up to Edinburgh to compete in a festival, and I'm pretty sure that my companies will be the only ones not being produced by someone with some professional experience.' They could see in the driving-mirror that she was frowning thoughtfully.

They were longing, all of them, to be able to say, 'Look—we'll come and give you a hand...' but the thought of the boys trekking round London, becoming more and more penniless, held them back.

There was a long silence, then Lyn said, 'Have you any special problems? Perhaps we might be able to help?'

'I say,' said the woman, 'I've got an idea. How about working for me for two or three weeks—just until the festival? I couldn't pay you much—a few pounds each—but I could put you up, so your keep wouldn't cost you anything. I've got a little house near Axminster. And then each of you could take charge of a company, and I could do the fourth. They've got producers already. All that is needed is someone to drop in and say the last word on tricky matters. What do you say to it?' They were too pleased to say much.

'It—it's too good to be true,' gulped Lyn. 'Why, we never expected to find work as quickly as this—but are you sure you can afford to pay three of us?'

'Yes, I think so.' She did a little calculating. 'I get a fairly large allowance for expenses, and I'll include you as expenses. I can pay you each four pounds a week for three weeks.'

Vicky clapped her hands. 'And we'll be able to send it nearly all to the boys. Oh, good! That'll keep them going for a few more weeks any rate.'

'Well, you'll really be doing me a kindness, because I am very much in need of help.'

'How perfectly lovely!' cried Lyn. 'We must write to Maddy tonight—and tell her to let the boys know.'

'Who is Maddy?' They explained about Maddy, and gave more details of themselves and their careers, to all of which their new friend listened attentively. Then she said, 'My name is Constance—Constance Felton. I do hope you'll be comfortable in my little house. I'm afraid I'll have to put one of you on a divan in the lounge.'

'Oh, that'll be fine,' said Lyn. 'I had the best night I've had for weeks last night, and that was in the back of a taxi.'

'And tomorrow I'll take you round to two of my dramatic clubs. One a school's and the other an adults'.'

'I shall feel awful, telling grown-up people what to do and not to do,' said Vicky.

'Oh, they'll be thrilled, and think you're wonderful when they know you're trained actresses,' Miss Felton assured them.

The little car purred on, covering mile after mile. They stopped for a late lunch at a country hotel, for which Miss Felton insisted on paying.

'You're on my pay-roll now,' she said. 'And you must think of those brothers of yours. All your pennies must go to them.'

'What a sweet person she is,' whispered Sandra to Lyn as they went for a wash after lunch. 'How *lucky* we are.'

'Yes. This is more the sort of luck we used to have, isn't it?' said Lyn. 'Let's hope it's turned for good.'

During the afternoon they became rather sleepy, and noticing this, Miss Felton stopped telling them about the one-act plays that were being entered for the contest and let them doze. In the late afternoon, when the scenery had changed to the beautiful hills and combes of Somerset, the car drew up outside a small seventeenth-century house, beautifully renovated, that stood in a paved garden by the side of the high road.

'Come in and we'll have something to eat,' said Miss Felton briskly as they got out. 'I'll put the car away afterwards.'

A tiny little birdlike woman in a check apron stood in the doorway.

'Back, then, Miss Constance...' she cried welcomingly.

'Yes, Lenny,' answered Miss Felton. 'And I've brought you some guests. Two for the blue room, and one for the divan. This is Mrs Leonard, my housekeeper.'

There was a high tea set out in a long low-ceilinged room, where a wood fire burned cheerily, and afterwards they were entertained by records on the radiogram from their hostess's fine collection. As soon as she saw them yawning she sent them to bed, saying, 'You must be in good form tomorrow, ready to meet a lot of wild amateurs.'

As Vicky rolled into bed she said, 'If this is what happens to hoboes, I'm glad I'm one.'

IO

NICK'S CAFF

It was the third day of the boys' search for Nick's Caff.

For sixteen hours of every day they had tramped the streets of London, exploring every alley-way, and inquiring in every restaurant for its whereabouts. Now they were sitting on a seat in Trafalgar Square, resting their weary feet.

'I don't believe there *is* such a place,' said Bulldog moodily. 'That silly old woman probably meant "Dick's Caff" or "Mick's Caff". Or perhaps it isn't even in the West End at all—'

'The infuriating part of it,' said Nigel, frowning, 'is that if only we could go to the police they would probably know it, if people of Lucky's type are in the habit of patronizing it.'

Jeremy fed some pigeons with the pieces of an old sandwich he had found in his pocket. 'Well, we can't go. Firstly, we're in this on our own, and secondly, because our parents just might have asked them to look out for us.'

'Where haven't we been?' inquired Bulldog, looking over Nigel's shoulder at the large-scale map of the West End that they had bought.

'There's a bit round King's Cross—if you call that West End—and a large patch around Covent Garden that is an absolute rabbit warren of little cafés.'

'Otherwise we've been everywhere?'

'I think so. We may have missed the odd street or two.'

'And Nick's Caff may be in one of those odd streets...' observed Jeremy. 'How are your feet?'

'Ghastly,' groaned Bulldog. 'I wish we'd got someone to darn our socks. Mine are gradually becoming a lot of holes joined together with strands of wool.'

'Perhaps Maddy would do them,' suggested Nigel.

'Worse than holes,' rejoined Jeremy. 'I've seen her darning. We'd never walk another step.'

'Which reminds me...' Nigel rose painfully to his feet. 'We'd better ring her. It's nearly five o'clock, and she'll have left the Academy if we don't look out.' They made their way to the phone-box and rang the number of the dramatic school. While they waited for her to be brought to the phone they could imagine very clearly what was going on. The secretary, whose voice they knew so well, would call out to a passing student, 'Find Madeline Fayne, please,' and that student would run up the wide stone steps shouting, 'Madeline Fayne—telephone...' and the cry would be taken up by the other students on all the flights of stairs.

'Madeline Fayne—telephone...' until at last it reached the ears of Maddy, who, if she was in a class, would excuse herself apologetically and fly down the stairs two or three at a time.

Oh, it made them feel miserable to imagine it all. 'Hullo,' came Maddy's voice, rather breathlessly.

'It's us,' said Nigel. 'Any news?'

'Yes.' Maddy was bubbling over with excitement. 'I had a letter from the girls this morning. And what do you think? They've got work!'

'*What?*'

'Yes! With a drama inspector or something. I'll send you the letter. Where are you staying now?'

'The Young Men's Hostel Association, Russell Square.'

'Sounds grim.'

'It's not too bad—and only a few bob a night.'

'And they've sent you some money.'

'Oh, good. Not that we're anywhere near spent out yet, but when we are, we shall be with a vengeance.'

Maddy said carelessly, 'Have you had any luck yet?'

'Not yet.'

'Oh, well, it's rather early to expect it, isn't it? May I come round with you this evening? I haven't any study to do.'

'If you think you can stand it.'

'Will you pick me up at the Academy?'

'No.' Nigel was definite about it. They could not bear to meet any of their ex-tutors or students that they knew, whose first question would be, 'Are you working?'

'Meet us outside Lyons, Tottenham Court Road, at about six o'clock. O.K.?'

'Right you are. And I'll bring the letter with me. Cheerio.'

They felt a little more cheerful, having spoken to Maddy, and heard good news of the girls.

'Well, they've fallen on their feet,' remarked Nigel.

'Trust them. They're just like cats. Quite nice ones, of course. But it looks as though they're going to be financing a fruitless search,' said Bulldog.

'Oh, come off it. We've only just started.'

'Thank goodness the weather hasn't been too bad. Imagine doing this in the rain.'

'What shall we do till we meet Maddy?'

'Nothing connected with walking,' stated Bulldog. 'Preferably something connected with lying down—with one's feet—up.' He lay back at full length on the seat to which they had returned, with his feet up on Nigel's knee. They were promptly pushed off again.

'It's cold sitting here,' grumbled Jeremy. 'Let's go into a News Cinema.'

'No,' said Nigel, 'we can't afford it.' Finally they ended up in the reading room of the St Martin's Street Library, ruefully reading the theatre magazines.

When they met Maddy at six o'clock she seemed to them to be looking incredibly young and bouncing and happy. She wore a cosy red winter coat, with a beret to match perched above her yellow pigtails.

'Can we go in here and eat?' was her first question.

'No,' said Nigel. 'We must eat at one of the cafés *en route*, to give us a chance to get into conversation about Nick's Caff. Come on. We'll do the King's Cross bit first.'

They walked and walked and walked, past the Florida Café, the Cosy Corner, 'La France', Café Philadelphia, every name under the sun. Maddy made a helpful and cheery companion, and although her legs were so much shorter than the others, she kept up with them manfully. They 'did' the King's Cross area, and then were rash and took a bus to the Strand, in order to begin the Covent Garden area.

'I wonder,' said Nigel, 'if it would be at all possible to trace Nick's Caff through the Licensed Victuallers what-not—'

'What what-not?' inquired Maddy.

'I don't really know *what* what-not—'

'Well, if you don't know what what-not, what good is it?'

They got off the bus and made their way along the dark streets of Covent Garden, looking into every lighted doorway. One café had no name on the door.

Maddy stepped inside. "Scuse me. What's the name of this place?' she asked the proprietor who stood behind the tea-urn.

'What's it to you?' he asked grudgingly.

'Oh, don't worry,' retorted Maddy, 'I haven't mistaken it for the Savoy.'

'Now look here you young—' But Bulldog squared his shoulders and stepped into the doorway beside her.

'We want to know,' he said menacingly, 'the name of this café.'

The proprietor cringed, noting the dangerous angle of Bulldog's hat. He had heard all about hold-up raids and blond accomplices.

'The Continental,' he said quickly. 'Step inside, do.'

'I wouldn't eat here,' said Maddy 'if it was the last place on earth and I was starving.' And she walked out, head in the air.

'All the same,' she said, when they were outside, 'let's eat soon. I'm ravenous. It's hungry work being a detective.'

'That's what we've found,' agreed Nigel, 'and food runs away with the money so.'

'Let's go into the cheapest place we can find.'

They went into a tiny café bearing the name 'The Lane Restaurant', which was in the shadow of Drury Lane Theatre. The theatre crowds were coming in and out, and the streets were full of large cars crawling through the narrow byways to pick up befurred and glittering passengers. They sat in the window of the little café watching it all, paying no attention to what was inside. The interior of the café was like the one they had first eaten in on their arrival in London on the furniture lorry, the same wooden tables and pews and steamy atmosphere. A few taxi-men came in for a quick cup of tea and hurried out again to their cabs. There was a game of cards going on amongst four rather shady-looking gentlemen in the corner.

'Doesn't it make you feel awful,' said Maddy. 'Seeing theatres emptying—and here we sit...'

At that moment a newcomer entered the café. He was tall and sturdy and wore a pin-stripe suit. As he swaggered up to the counter he stared at the Blue Doors suspiciously. The proprietor, a bent wizened little man, stood up and said, 'Good evening, stranger.'

'Hi ya, Nick,' was the laconic answer.

'Yes, it does make one feel awful, doesn't it?' Mechanically Jeremy answered Maddy's question. Then he jumped as if he'd been stung. The others were sitting spellbound, gazing at the little man behind the counter.

'Did you hear what I heard?' inquired Jeremy softly.

'Yes,' whispered Maddy. 'He called him Nick—'

'I wonder if—if that means—' They were talking in whispers, with their heads together, their eyes wide with hope.

'We must ask—'

'Who'll ask?'

'I'll handle this.' Nigel rose, carrying his teacup, and sauntered up to the counter.

''Nother cup o' char—please,' he said, and leaned up against the counter beside the burly man. While the urn was steaming and spitting, Nigel continued, 'Never knew this place was called "The Lane Restaurant".'

'Never is,' said the little man shortly, stirring sugar into the tea with a teaspoon attached to the counter by a length of string. Nigel willed him to continue. He did so.

'Bin called Nick's Caff ever since I've bin here. Not that my name's Nick—it's not. It's Bill. And the bloke wot 'ad it before me was known as Nick—but 'is name was Stanislaus. I dunno—someone 'ere must'a bin called Nick at some time or other—twopence, please.' Nigel gave him sixpence, ignored the change, and offered him a cigarette. The large customer was still eyeing him suspiciously.

'Seen Lucky lately?' Nigel asked carelessly. At the table in the window Maddy and the two boys were not watching, but were straining their ears to catch the reply. Nick looked for a long time at Nigel. Nigel was very conscious that his overcoat was all wrong for a friend of Lucky's, and his tie too quiet.

'No,' said Nick shortly. 'He ain't been round 'ere.' And he resumed his conversation with the big man about how much he had lost on the dogs last week. Nigel returned to the table with his cup of tea.

'Well,' he said quietly, 'we've found Nick's Caff. But it doesn't seem to have helped us. He's not been here lately.' They said nothing. As always in this quest, once they had found the thing that they had been hunting down for a long time, it seemed to take them no nearer their goal.

Then Jeremy said, 'Well, he's bound to come here some time. And if we hang around long enough, we're bound to see him.'

'Yes,' said Bulldog. 'We must stay here from opening time to closing time, in shifts.'

'Night-shifts or short shifts?' inquired Maddy, but no-one would laugh.

'Gosh, what a place to have to spend your life in,' said Jeremy.

'And we shall spend a fortune in cups of tea—'

'But we must try to get on the right side of Nick,' said Nigel. 'I'm sure he could help us more. What's the time?'

'Nearly ten.'

'You must go, Maddy,' ordered Nigel. 'You ought to have been back at your digs hours ago. Mrs Bosham will be worried.'

'But—but Lucky might come in any moment,' she expostulated.

'We'll ring you if he does,' promised Jeremy. 'Look, I'd better take her home, hadn't I?'

'Yes,' agreed Nigel. 'And come back for us here.' Still grumbling, Maddy was led away.

'What time does this joint close?' inquired Bulldog. Nigel pointed to a notice on the wall that read, 'Open seven a.m. till midnight.'

'Gosh, that'll be hard work.'

'There must always be two of us on—just in case,' said Nigel.

The door-bell clanged continuously. Taxi-men, chorus girls, market workers from Covent Garden, every kind of person imaginable—but no Lucky. They were still sitting over their third cups of tea when Jeremy returned.

'Maddy insists on coming here tomorrow evening to do her shift. She says if she's got any work to do she'll bring it with her.'

III

Nigel laughed. 'I'd like to see Maddy learning Shakespeare in these surroundings.'

Eventually it was closing time, and the three boys were the last to leave.

'Be seeing you...' Nigel called out to Nick, who was yawning and rubbing his eyes.

And he did see them. Every day and all day, for three long weeks, two at least of them were sitting in Nick's Caff. They had breakfast, lunch and tea and dinner there, and in between were endless cups of tea—strong and black—from chipped cups. They got so unable to face it that in desperation they turned to coffee. But that was worse—made from essence and tinned milk.

At first Nick eyed them with suspicion. He could not place them. But then he grew used to them. It often happened like that. People adopted his café as a haunt for several weeks, and were there continually, using it as a meeting place, an office, a second home, and then for no apparent reason, they would disappear completely, only to turn up again unaccountably a few weeks, months or years later. These youngsters were evidently another example of it. For the first few days they kept their eyes on the door, their hearts leaping every time the bell clanged, but soon their optimism faded and they sat back reading newspapers, doing the crossword puzzle, waiting for it to be time to slip out for a few hours' fresh air. Maddy became quite a favourite with the other regular customers. Sometimes she even helped Nick with the washing up. One of the taxi-men would drop in during the slack period of the evening, about half past eight, and hear her lines for the next day's verse speaking or diction. After a time he became quite a Shakespeare fan, and one evening he and Maddy and Jeremy went off on a jaunt to see a performance at the Old Vic from the gallery. But that was the extent of their outings during those weeks for their funds were slowly disappearing, although the girls were sending as much as they could each week. They began to get very despondent and liverish through sitting about so much.

'It's quite obvious that he'll never come here again,' growled Bulldog. 'At least, not till he's spent all our money.'

Lately, Nick had got into the habit of coming and sitting with them between serving customers. He was never very talkative, but seemed to like their company. Sometimes they casually mentioned Lucky in conversation in a friendly sort of way, hoping that he might make some comment, but it never worked. Tonight, while Nick was at the table, they tried it on again.

'Look,' said Bulldog suddenly, pointing out of the window, 'isn't that old Lucky over the road?' The others pretended to peer out of the window in an interested fashion, but Nick did not even bother to look.

'No,' he said. 'Wouldn't be 'im.' They swung round, dropping their pretence.

'Why not?' said Nigel tensely.

''E's gorn into the country.'

'How do you know?'

'Saw 'im yesterday. Meant to tell you. You know when I went out last evening to see my daughter-in-law orf at Paddington? Well, who should I bump into on the platform but Lucky Green. Said he was goin' to Cornwall or somewhere by the night train. On a job, I think.'

'Cornwall?'

'Think so. Or was it Devon? Well, down that way.' With one accord they rose. Nigel threw five bob on the table. 'Thanks a lot, Nick. And thanks for the hospitality.'

They were out in the street in a flash. Nigel hailed a taxi, and they piled in.

'We want to go to Paddington. But first we want to pick up some luggage at the Young Men's Hostel in Russell Square. Quickly, please. Do you know when there's a night train to Cornwall?'

'Ten thirty, I believe,' said the taxi-man. 'But you'll have to move to catch it.'

'What about me? What about me?' Maddy was inquiring at the top of her voice. 'Can I come too?'

'No, of course not,' Nigel told her. 'You must stay here to maintain communications.'

They ran up the stairs of the hostel, flung their clothes into their grips, hastily paid the bill and ran down to the taxi, which dashed through the busy streets to the station.

'We'll send you a wire, Maddy, if we find any address where you can get in touch with us. We may see the girls, too, if we get time.'

'Funny he should go down this way, isn't it?' said Jeremy.

'My goodness, can we afford the fare?' asked Bulldog. They hastily counted up. They would just about be able to do it, with very little left over. As they arrived on the station the whistle for the Cornwall express was just blowing. They dashed through the barrier, ignoring the ticket collector, and jumped on as it began to move.

'Where are you for?' shouted the guard.

'Don't know,' yelled Bulldog, waving his atrocious hat to Maddy.

'Bring him back alive,' shouted Maddy, waving her beret.

'Have you got a platform ticket, miss?' asked the ticket collector weakly.

II

VILLAGE DRAMA

The school hall of Little Heseltine was tiny, smaller than the Blue Door Theatre. The village only consisted of a church, a school, two inns, a shop and a cluster of thatched cottages.

'How funny to go to school here,' remarked Vicky as the car drew up outside.

'How many pupils are there, Miss Felton?' asked Lyn.

'Only twenty. And ten of them are in the play.'

'Don't the other ten feel bad about it?' Lyn wanted to know.

'Yes. But they can't be in it because they live so far away that they can't stay for the late rehearsals like the ones from the village. Ah, here's Miss Presto.' A brown-faced lady of uncertain age with dark hair wound round her head in a coronet had come to the gate. She greeted Miss Felton warmly, looking surprised at seeing the three girls.

'Yes, I've got some visitors for you today, Miss Presto. Three real actresses...' Miss Presto's mouth formed an 'O' of surprise, and her dark brows disappeared into her hair-line. 'They've come to give us advice about the play, then one of them will adopt you and drop in every day until the festival.'

'How splendid!' cried Miss Presto. 'The children *will* be pleased.'

They were led into the schoolroom, where twenty desks were arranged in rows, and filled with a medley of girls and boys from four to fourteen or fifteen who all goggled at the sight of the Blue Doors. Round the walls there was a brightly coloured frieze, and on the blackboard a picture of a windmill that all the pupils were copying on to their drawing boards.

'Here's Miss Felton, children,' cried Miss Presto. 'Say good morning to her.'

'Good morning, Miss Felton,' they chorused in a broad West Country burr.

'Well, it's time for rehearsal of the play, so those not in it can go out and get on with the gardens.'

'Can't we watch, miss?' asked a timid voice.

'No—you're all going to be the audience at the dress rehearsal, aren't you? Now off you go.' When they had gone, with a scuffle of boots and a banging of desk lids, Miss Presto announced to the remainder, 'Now these three young ladies are professional actresses who have come to see your play today, and they are going to give us their advice and criticism, so do your best, children. And no books today. You all know it perfectly well.'

The desks were pushed to the side of the room to make a space large enough for a stage, and after a lot of chatter and giggling and squabbling, the children were manoeuvred into their correct positions for the beginning of the play, and the two teachers and the Blue Doors settled into chairs in front of them.

It was a rough and unpolished one-act play about the Restoration period, and at times the girls found it very hard not to laugh. The West Country dialect was so wrong for the courtiers they were supposed to represent. And yet these children had amazing sincerity and enthusiasm. The three girls were brimming over with ideas for how the performance could be improved, and at the end of it, the lists they had drawn up were extensive. They worked with the cast all the morning and most of the afternoon, and by tea-time there was a noticeable improvement. They had tea at a cottage in the village.

'And now,' said Miss Felton, 'for the adults.'

After a drive of twenty miles or so they came to a British Legion hall, where a group of twelve or fifteen were rehearsing a modern mystery play. To start with, it was very badly written, and secondly, the producer knew very little about producing. The Blue Doors writhed in agony, wondering how they could phrase their criticisms tactfully.

'Not very good, is it?' whispered Miss Felton. They had to admit it was not. When it was over there was rather a horrible silence. Then Lyn took the situation in hand.

'Now, shall we all start off again slowly, and we'll discuss every line as we go...' It was hard going, for the actors all had their own ideas about their roles—for the most part quite mistaken ideas. It was very, very difficult without seeming rude, to criticize these people, old enough to be their mothers and fathers. And by the time the rehearsal was over the Blue Doors were exhausted with the struggle against inexperience and bad producing.

And so it went on for several weeks. Lyn was given charge of the adult group, and went to their hall by bus every evening.

Vicky had Miss Presto's school children, and Sandra another group who were doing a musical play.

The last looked as if it was going to be the most successful, for some of the children had beautiful natural voices, and under Sandra's tuition they improved daily. The little house at Axminster with Miss Felton and her faithful Lenny was cosy and friendly and they loved to return there at night after a long cold drive home, either by car or bumpy country bus. Constance Felton talked to them a lot about her life and ambitions.

'There's a wonderful satisfaction in teaching—teaching anything,' she said one night as they sat over their coffee and sandwiches by the firelight. 'It's almost like being a potter—moulding things out of very rough clay.' She smiled. 'You probably think that the finished vessels aren't much to boast about, but although I know that very few of the people in my district, children or adults, have any outstanding dramatic ability, yet I know that since I have been here I have, to a degree, broadened their outlooks by introducing them to the great poets and dramatists.'

'It is wonderful,' said Lyn, 'when you've been struggling with a scene for hours, and are just at the point of losing your temper and giving the whole thing up, when suddenly—like magic—it all comes right and you feel you could fling your arms around the necks of the whole cast, out of sheer gratitude—'

'If only one of my four companies could get somewhere in the contest,' sighed Miss Felton.

'Perhaps Sandra's group will,' said Vicky. 'It's a charming little play.'

'All except that wretched little Terence Godbold with those dreadful adenoids.'

'Yes, did he *have* to be in it?' inquired Sandra.

'Well, he looked so angelic,' said Miss Felton apologetically. 'No-one else could possibly take the part of Cupid.'

'I know,' said Sandra, jumping up suddenly. 'Let's cut his lines, and make him mime them. It will be quite effective, and save him using that awful voice. Look—where's the script?' And they were at work again.

Lyn had the most tricky job, for the adults were much more difficult to organize than the children. She could never be sure that they would all attend rehearsals, for sometimes one would be working late, another evening someone else's children would be ill, and on occasions people would not turn up because they were 'too tired'. After the rigorous discipline of the dramatic school and professional rep., this attitude amazed and infuriated Lyn.

'If they don't want to rehearse, why do they join in the first place?' she would demand of the producer, who was a rather trying and fluttery woman called Christabel Skate.

'Well, you see, my dear, *they* think of it as an amusement, not as a *religion*, as you and I do.'

Miss Skate had once toured as a 'singing lady' in a Gilbert and Sullivan opera company, many many years ago, and on this count she was considered in the village to be the High Priestess of Drama. Her fringe, and large bun on the back of her head, her jade ear-rings, hand-painted beads and floating chiffon shawls, added to her reputation. Unfortunately, however much she may or may not have known about the stage, she had the unhappy knack of saying precisely the wrong thing to everybody. Her ideas of producing had been gleaned from rather arty-crafty books on the subject, borrowed from the County library, and these ideas she put into practice, regardless of everything. It was said that she once kept Mrs Trevelyan, the butcher's wife who was more than a little on the plump side, lying for half an hour on the floor of the British Legion hall with a book balanced on her extensive diaphragm, teaching her to 'breathe properly', while the rest of the cast hung round fretting and fuming at the waste of rehearsal time.

As soon as the company got used to the thought of being directed by a 'slip of a girl' like Lyn, they welcomed her good sense and tactful approach, and realized that she would be the saving of the play. Miss Skate adored her, and thought that everything she did and said was perfect.

'It is so wonderful,' she would cry ecstatically, 'to have someone to talk to who speaks one's own language. I realize now that I have been *starved*—mentally, of course—for years.' But sometimes Lyn would find it very hard to bear Miss Skate's well-meaning blunders.

'Now just think,' Lyn would say to one of the actors, concerning some situation in the play, 'how *you* would feel if that were to happen to *you*—in your own life.'

'Ah, yes,' Miss Skate would breathe. 'The Stanislavsky theory— emotion memory, as he calls it...' And immediately the simple country folk would shy away, frightened by the 'fancy talk' and positive that it meant something extremely complicated and beyond them.

And then there was the matter of Mrs Trevelyan. For some unknown reason she was playing the part of the heroine, a young girl of twenty-one. Now, Mrs Trevelyan was good for forty or more, and no light weight. When Lyn inquired from Miss Skate why Mrs Trevelyan should be playing the heroine the reply was merely a vague, 'Oh, she always does.' But from some other members of the company she gathered that Mrs Trevelyan was a very liberal subscriber to the funds of the company, and for this reason it was taken for granted that she should take the chief part in every production. Lyn racked her brains for days to know how to approach Mrs Trevelyan to suggest that she played an older part.

'I keep hoping she'll fall down and sprain her ankle, or get influenza,' she confessed to Sandra, 'but she's as strong as a horse—and looks like one. Whatever can I do? They just *can't* go in for the competition with her playing that part.'

Then Fate came to Lyn's aid. An elderly woman who was playing the part of the grandmother went down with jaundice, and immediately there was panic to know how to fill her place.

'I think,' said Miss Skate, 'that although I do not feel the part is really *me*—I shall have to play it.'

'Oh, no, Miss Skate,' Lynette put in hastily, 'you are much too valuable as a producer. It is impossible to see a play in the right—the right perspective—if you are also taking part.'

'Ah, yes. The dear girl is so right. How she knows her theatre,' sighed Miss Skate.

'What we want,' said Lyn loudly, so that all the rest of the cast could not possibly miss hearing it, 'is someone with that little extra flair for character. It's so very much more difficult and *interesting* a part than a straight one. And the right person in it could steal the show—Mrs Trevelyan!' she cried, appearing to be struck suddenly by a brilliant idea, 'how about you? You're a quick study—I believe that you could save the situation. After all, the part you're playing now is a very ordinary one, isn't it? I think you could do wonders for the grandmother.'

Mrs Trevelyan looked surprised. 'But what about my part?'

'Oh, little Jennifer could easily slip into that.' Jennifer was a young girl of sixteen or seventeen who was at the moment acting as prompter. She looked up hopefully, flushing with pleasure.

'You see, Mrs Trevelyan, anyone can play a straight juvenile, but it takes someone with a little—well—*weight* to play a character part.' Although Lyn kept a straight face, she could not help giggling inwardly at her own choice of words. But fortunately Mrs Trevelyan did not see any double meaning in them, and her face brightened.

'Oh, yes,' she said. 'I think I could manage—if you're sure it won't matter my part being given to someone else.'

'No, I think you will be doing us all a good turn by taking over such a tricky part—at such short notice, I mean—I think that the judges at the contest should be informed of it.' Mrs Trevelyan beamed with pleasure and Jennifer adored Lyn for ever after. Miss Skate enveloped Lyn in an embrace that ground her against rows of hand-painted beads.

'My tactful little creature!' she cried. 'Now why can't poor Christabel handle people like that?'

Lyn arrived home exhausted.

'I envy you two,' she said to Sandra and Vicky. 'You can just say firmly to your kids, "No, you don't do that part properly," and give it to someone else, but I have to think up a whole tissue of lies if I want to alter the casting.'

They were lounging in the dimly lit cottage bedroom that Vicky and Sandra shared, and Lyn was trying to muster enough energy to depart to the divan. Sandra, who sat brushing her hair at the dressing-table, stopped suddenly with the brush still poised in the air.

'I say,' she said. 'I think I've discovered something.'

'Where?' the other two demanded in alarm.

'Or rather—somebody. A kid in my play. She wasn't there the day you saw it, when we first went over. She was away ill, and only turned up last week. Her singing voice is very bad—she only sings in the chorus—but the other day I was trying to make them pronounce the words clearly, and I asked one of them to *say* the lines of a song that the chorus of Greek maidens has to sing. And she recited several verses in the most beautiful speaking voice— very deep and soft, with only a slight accent that was really an added attraction. And she's a lovely girl—quite outstanding. Very long dark hair and extremely blue eyes, and fair skin.'

'How old?'

'About fourteen, I think. But the teacher says that she's dreamy and bad at lessons, and attends school very irregularly—'

'Sounds as though she's got the makings of an actress then,' said Lyn wryly. 'What's her name?'

'It's a beautiful name—Zillah Pendray.'

'Phew!' whistled Vicky. 'That sounds too much like Hollywood to be true.'

'I know. Some of these kids have got extraordinary names—at the other end of the scale we have Pansy Fish!'

'*No*, I don't believe it—'

'Yes, it's quite true. And so is Zillah. I have a feeling about her. I'd like you both to come and have a look at her when you've got time.'

'I can come any day during the day-time,' said Lyn.

'I *can't* come any day-time, except Wednesday,' said Vicky.

'Let's go on Wednesday then,' said Lynette. 'I'm anxious to see this discovery of yours.'

'I hope you'll like her—of course, you may think she's ghastly— vacant-looking in fact. But I think she's unusual.'

At this moment there was a knock on the door, and in came Mrs Leonard with a tray loaded with steaming hot beakers of cocoa, home-made jam tarts and cheese straws.

'Oh, how heavenly,' cried Lyn. 'You do believe in feeding us up, don't you?'

The cheery little woman beamed at them. 'I do that, Miss Lynette. You're all three nothing but a drink o' water. And no-one can ever say they've stayed in my house and not gone away fatter than when they came.' And out she went, leaving them munching away happily.

Before long Miss Felton came in, back late from a meeting in Axminster. She, too, joined the cocoa party, and warmed herself beside the bedroom fire.

'Sandra's been telling us about a discovery of hers—Zillah someone or other—'

Miss Felton wrinkled her brows. 'Oh, yes—the Pendray girl. She's a strange type. I can never quite make her out. There was some trouble about her being in the play, I believe. Her parents don't want her to be. But apparently they're letting her now, on the condition that she doesn't go up to Edinburgh for the contest, isn't that right, Sandra? Still, she won't be much loss to you. She doesn't sing very well, does she?'

'No,' said Sandra, 'but you should hear her speaking voice.'

'I don't think I ever have.'

'Come over with us on Wednesday then,' said Lyn.

'We're going to look her over.'

'Yes, I will,' said Miss Felton. 'Pass the cheese straws, please, Vicky. More cocoa, Lyn?'

'Yes, and a jam tart please...'

12

FARMHOUSE TEA

'We've come in full force today,' laughed Miss Felton, as the four of them entered the schoolroom at Polgarth where Sandra's musical play was about to be rehearsed. Lyn and Vicky immediately looked round for the girl Sandra had described. There was no doubt as to which she was, although she stood with her back to them gazing out of the window. The poise of her head, the long curling dark hair and her strange graceful carriage marked her as one apart from the clumsy, shouting, giggling children who were running around trying to arrange the furniture for the play. And when she turned to face them, they caught their breaths. Her complexion was fair, with vivid colouring, and her eyes were of the bluest blue imaginable.

'Well,' whispered Lyn to Vicky.

'Isn't she amazing?'

'Yes. But is she always like that?'

'That's the trouble. She is. That's why I was afraid she might strike you as being vacant.'

'She is—but it's rather attractive.'

'Wait till you hear her speak...'

'Now then, children,' Sandra clapped her hands in such a schoolmistressish fashion that Lyn and Vicky exchanged amused glances. 'Let's get started. Show Miss Felton how much you've improved since she was here last.'

The onlookers paid little attention to the play, but watched Zillah Pendray closely. Her every movement made a picture, but her face was as strangely empty as a sleep walker's. Then Sandra clapped her hands again.

'No, no!' she said, 'I didn't hear a word of that verse. Zillah, will you please *say* the words clearly, so that we can all hear them.'

Zillah obeyed. They were jingling and unimportant lines, in a play that was consciously 'a charming play for children', but as she spoke them they sounded like sheer poetry.

Lyn's mouth fell open. 'That voice...' she whispered to Vicky, 'and we've been pegging away at voice production all these years... And she's got it naturally.'

'And only a very slight accent—it's amazing,' Vicky agreed.

'The next verse, Zillah, please,' Sandra said. The girl looked at her levelly, then continued with a rather bored expression as though her thoughts were elsewhere.

'Yes,' said Sandra to the other children when Zillah had finished, 'and now let us hear the words as clearly as that when you are singing.'

For the rest of the rehearsal Lyn's head was in a whirl. She knew that she wanted to do something about this strangely talented girl, but did not quite know what.

'It's not right,' she thought to herself, 'that she should be wasted in a backwater like Polgarth. She'll probably grow up and marry the blacksmith—if there is one—and that lovely voice and everything might just as well never have been. And yet, is it right to meddle in other people's lives?' At the same time she suffered a feeling of envy at meeting someone so well equipped for a career as an actress, but obviously without any idea of ever becoming one.

After the rehearsal was finished, Sandra called Zillah over to them. 'I want you to meet Miss Halford and Miss Darwin. You weren't here when they came last time, were you?' The girl did not reply, but just inclined her head towards them in a manner of greeting.

'Well, Zillah,' said Lynette. 'What are you going to do when you leave school?'

She shrugged her shoulders.

'Help on your father's farm, eh?' said Miss Felton, trying to draw her out.

'Perhaps so.'

'Isn't there anything else you'd like to do?'

A slight shade of life crept into the girl's face. 'Yes, miss, I'd like to go to Axminster—'

'Oh, yes?'

'And work in Woolly's.'

They were flabbergasted, and did not know whether to laugh or shake her.

'All right, off you go, Zillah,' said Miss Felton, and they exchanged despairing looks.

'To work in Woolworth's...' repeated Lyn in a dazed manner. 'Why, it would be like—like seeing Helen of Troy in the Home and Colonial.'

'I think that her parents will keep her at home,' said Miss Felton, 'if I have summed them up correctly.'

'Well, it will be a wicked thing to do,' said Lyn heatedly, 'to waste that voice—and those looks—either on a lot of cows and pigs or behind a counter at Woolworth's.'

'Do you mean,' said Vicky, 'that she ought to be an actress?'

'Of course I do. And that's what made Sandra bring us to see her, isn't it?'

'Yes,' said Sandra, 'I suppose it was. But look here, we don't know that she can act, do we? We've only heard her reciting those lines perfectly straightforwardly. There's a difference between having a lovely voice and knowing how to act, isn't there?'

'Well,' said Lynette, 'how do we find out? Do you know, Miss Felton?'

'No,' she admitted 'Zillah has always seemed so apathetic that I've never bothered to give her a decent part in anything. I've always chosen someone a little more vivacious.'

'That's the trouble,' frowned Lyn. 'She seems so vague—she might almost be half-witted.'

'You can ask Miss Presto about her life, if you like,' suggested Miss Felton, but all that the teacher could say was that Zillah was dull and inattentive, and her parents kept her at home whenever they thought they would.

As they drank their tea in the little drawing-room of the school house, their thoughts were full of what they could do to find out more about this strange and bewildering creature. Miss Felton was deep in conversation with the schoolmistress about plans for the expedition to Edinburgh, and she said to the girls, 'Look, I shall be about another three-quarters of an hour if you want to go out and explore the village.'

'Yes, perhaps we will—before it gets dark.'

Polgarth was a tiny little village consisting of one street and a few scattered houses that thinned out into wild and desolate countryside. Vicky and Sandra amused themselves by looking into the window of the one draper's shop, where very ugly and old-fashioned garments were labelled with tickets that read *Very Special* and *The Latest Thing*. They were arguing over the merits of two particularly repulsive hats, one marked '*très chic*, fifteen and eleven' and the other '*à la mode*, six and ninepence halfpenny,' so Lynette wandered off down the road and soon found herself on the outskirts of the village. In the distance she could hear the sea washing against the cliffs so she quickened her pace, anxious to reach it. It was beginning to get dark, and a strong breeze blew against her. Then, quite suddenly, she found herself in view of the sea which lay below her, roaring and dashing against jagged rocks. She stood for a long time looking at the sea and the dark hurrying clouds, wondering how the boys were getting on in their search for Lucky, and then with a sigh turned to make her way back to the village. Then she stopped again, and peered into the distance along the cliff top to her left. A figure was standing on a flat boulder, pointing a finger out to sea, then turning and gesticulating, as if addressing a large crowd. Even before she was near enough to see clearly who it was, Lynette felt certain that she knew.

As she approached she saw that her feeling had been right. It was Zillah who stood on the flat piece of rock declaiming to an imaginary audience. She had taken her coat off and fastened it round her shoulders like a cloak, and the wind streamed her long hair out round her face. What it was that she was saying,

Lynette could not hear for the sound of the waves and the wind, but she stared open-mouthed at the change that had come over the girl. Her cheeks were bright, her eyes flashed, and the changing expressions on her face were full of deep emotion. Drawing her cloak around her and turning seawards she suddenly saw Lyn, and stood transfixed. Then a slow blush spread over her face and she turned to run.

'No, no. Don't go! Zillah, come here a minute.'

Lynette hurried over the uneven rocky ground towards her. Zillah halted, and turned to look fearfully at her like a frightened animal. When Lynette found herself face to face with the girl she did not quite know what to say. They stood looking at each other, both rather out of breath from exertion in the strong wind. Then Zillah said rebelliously, 'I'm not barmy—'

'I didn't think for a minute that you were. I was just—interested in what you were doing.'

Zillah hung her head, shamefaced. 'It's a game,' she mumbled, then looked up defensively.

'Oh, I know I'm too old for stuff like that—kids' games, my Mum and Dad keep telling me—'

'But I'm not telling you that,' said Lynette eagerly. 'I'm very interested. Why, I used to play pretence games until I was quite old—much older than you—until it turned into acting. But I was luckier than you. I had other people to play them with.'

'I don't want anyone else,' said Zillah sulkily. 'The other kids laugh at me. And everyone says I'm dull—'

'So you go on with the games—inside your head—all the time, so that no-one knows—'

'That's right. But sometimes I break out, like today.'

'Where do you live?' asked Lyn. 'I'll walk with you.' Zillah pointed to a grey farmhouse in the distance. 'Over there.' Lyn fell into step beside her.

'You know, Zillah, where we were studying in London, they used to have one lesson that you'd have liked. It was called "Improvisation". The teacher would give us some vague outline of a plot and we had to get up and act it, making up the lines as we went along. Now, what you were acting just now was the sort of thing that we used to do. What exactly was the plot of the scene you were doing?'

'Well...' Zillah began shyly, then stopped. 'No, miss. You'll laugh at me.'

'To me it looked rather like a bit of *King Lear*.'

Zillah looked vague. 'No, I wasn't a king, I was a princess. And a lot of enemies had got hold of me and were going to throw me into the sea, and I was—I was just making a farewell speech,' she finished up lamely.

'Rather a good idea,' said Lyn.

Suddenly the girl took hold of Lyn's wrist, looked at her watch, then gave an exclamation of horror.

'Oh, I'm behind again—my Mum will be raving...' And she started to run.

'Hey, Zillah! We'll call round and see you tomorrow afternoon when you've got home from school.'

'Oh...' Zillah looked as though she wanted to say, 'No, please don't,' but without a word she raced away. Lyn hurried back to the others and told them excitedly what had happened.

'She was terrific,' she said. 'If only you could have seen her! She was completely un-self-conscious—and as full of life as you could imagine. I couldn't hear what she was saying—it was probably rot—but she looked terrific! And with that voice—oh, gosh, we've made a discovery!'

'But what can we do about it? Does she want to be an actress?'

'Does she *want* to be? She is one—but she doesn't know it. She calls it "playing" and is ashamed to enjoy anything so childish. Apparently her parents have tried to stamp it out of her. I'm going to see them tomorrow. Coming?'

'Oh, we *can't*,' said Sandra. 'What right have we to interfere?'

'Listen,' said Lyn. 'We're teaching down here, aren't we? We run a theatre, don't we? Or rather—didn't we? And we've been to a dramatic school? Surely we should know if someone has got real talent or not. If you'd seen her this afternoon... At any rate, I'm calling there tomorrow, if only to see what her home surroundings are like.'

'I'll come too,' said Vicky, 'out of sheer curiosity. Come on, Sandra. It'll be fun.'

Sandra shook her head pessimistically. 'I think it will prove rather sticky.'

The next afternoon, a little while after Polgarth school had turned out, the three girls walked resolutely towards the farmhouse that Zillah had indicated. As they drew nearer, they saw that it was a grey rambling building, surrounded by sheds and outhouses.

'Looks rather a dreary sort of place, doesn't it?' observed Lyn.

'I always thought it would be rather nice to live on a farm,' said Vicky.

When they knocked on the highly polished brass door knocker it echoed hollowly through the house. Zillah answered it, looking rather scared.

'We've come to see you,' said Lynette.

'Yes,' said Zillah rather tremulously. 'You'd better come in.' She showed them into a spotlessly clean drawing-room where every antimacassar was snowy white, and the potted ferns in the window were arranged in meticulous rows. It was the most un-lived-in room they had ever seen.

'I bet this is only used for weddings and funerals,' observed Sandra. Then Zillah's mother came in. She was a pale-faced woman, wearing an old-fashioned black dress, and with a frightened expression. She looked at the three girls as though she had never seen anything like them before. Zillah lurked behind her in the doorway.

Lyn rose and held out her hand. 'How do you do, Mrs Pendray. I do hope that you don't mind us descending on you like this.'

'Pleased to meet you,' murmured Mrs Pendray, taking Lyn's hand and nodding nervously at the other two.

'You see,' went on Lyn, 'I had a talk with Zillah yesterday, and well—we've all been very interested in her after seeing her in the school play, so we thought we'd like to come and see you about her.'

'Not been getting into any trouble at the school, has she?'

'Oh, no! And we're hardly in a position to care, if she had. You see, Mrs Pendray, we're not teachers, we're actresses really'— Mrs Pendray looked at them uncomfortably, as if Lyn had said something embarrassing—'and that is why we're interested in your daughter.'

'Ay, she's a good-looking lass, I know.' Mrs Pendray seemed stung into life. 'But we don't want her head filled with a lot of nonsense. She's a difficult enough child as it is—lazy and slummocky—and as idle as they come. So if it's for this acting business you're wanting her, miss, I'll tell you straightways her dad and I won't hear of her doing any more of it. Gallivanting off to Edinburgh, indeed! There's enough to do about this place to keep six women busy, let alone the two of us. All this schooling takes up the girl's time. Why, she's nigh on fourteen now, and at her age I was running a home and looking after nine little brothers and sisters...' She had to stop for breath.

'My goodness! Were you really?' said Lynette. 'That must have been quite a handful. But your daughter is very clever too, Mrs Pendray. Only in a different way.'

Mrs Pendray sniffed. 'First I've heard of it. All the other teachers say she's dull.'

'She has a very beautiful voice.'

'Beautiful voice? Why, she can't keep in tune for two minutes.'

'I mean a speaking voice. And she has looks and imagination. And those are very important things—if you're going to be an actress.'

Mrs Pendray looked round at the three of them in horrified amazement. 'Do you mean—for life?'

Lyn smiled at the phrasing. 'Yes, Mrs Pendray, for life. For a living.'

Mrs Pendray turned to her daughter. 'Zillah,' she said shortly. 'Go outside.' Zillah disappeared like a shadow.

'Listen, miss. No doubt you're thinking you're trying to help our girl. But we know what she's worth, and very little that is. And we are trying to bring her up as a good God-fearing girl, and get rid of all this stupid dreamy nonsense she's got in that head of hers. So I'll thank you kindly for the interest you've shown, and ask you to let well alone.'

Lyn blushed, feeling very snubbed, and looked round at the others.

'Oh, well,' said Sandra, getting up hurriedly, 'then we won't trouble you any longer—'

But Mrs Pendray unbent slightly. 'Now please don't think I'm meaning to be unneighbourly. I'd be glad if you'd have a bite of tea with us while you're here.' Sandra frowned at Lyn, hoping she would refuse, but, seeing the more kindly expression on the woman's face had given Lyn fresh hope.

'That's very kind. We'd love a cup of tea.' But when they were shown into the large farm kitchen, it was more than a cup of tea that was set out on the table. There were large golden loaves of home-made bread, a slab of rich farm butter, large pastry flans, Cornish pasties and an enormous apple pie. The girls stared in amazement.

'Now make yourselves at home, do. Her dad'll be in in a minute, so I'll ask you not to mention that you're—theatricals.' She lowered her voice as though she were saying 'convicts'. They agreed, and sat down at the table. The kitchen was a much pleasanter room than the drawing-room, and the delicious tea warmed them up and made them feel more kindly disposed towards Zillah's mother. Zillah waited on them silently, running back and forth into the scullery for hot water.

'What wonderful pastry,' observed Sandra.

'That's Zillah's make—that's mine.' There was no difference between them, and the girls looked at Zillah admiringly. Perhaps there was something in her mother's idea of upbringing after all.

Then the back door slammed and in strode Mr Pendray. He was a giant of a man with bushy bristling eyebrows, a tanned heavy face and a thatch of grizzled hair. His rough working clothes suited him so well that one could not imagine him wearing anything else. He stopped in surprise at the sight of the three girls.

'These are the three young ladies from the school. They've been helping out,' said Mrs Pendray with careful truth.

'How d'y do,' he said gruffly, and sat down at the table, obviously wondering what they were doing in his house. Lyn looked at him calculatingly. After all—she had only promised not to say that they were on the stage themselves.

'We are very interested in Zillah,' she began. Mrs Pendray, Zillah and the other girls looked up in alarm.

'Oh, yes?' He sounded suspicious already.

'We—we think she ought to go on the stage.' Lyn's voice trembled slightly.

There was a long pause and then he said with ominous calm, 'Oh, y'do, do you? And might I ask why?'

'Well—she has a lovely voice, looks and imagination, and well...' Lyn trailed off, terrified by the anger in his eyes.

'And now *I'll* tell *you* why she's not going to. Our Zillah may be dull but she's a good girl, and we're trying to bring her up to be useful and ladylike, and that's as much as a girl needs. Stage, indeed—why they're nothing but a lot of painted—'

'Father—' broke in Mrs Pendray, but he swept on.

'Painted good-for-nothings. I wouldn't have my daughter associate with such folk for a fortune. Why, I wouldn't have an actress set foot in my house.' Lyn, Sandra and Vicky stole glances at each other, hardly able to believe their ears. Vicky looked round for the door in case they had to make a hasty exit. Zillah and Mrs Pendray showed signs of distress but the farmer took no notice.

'It's all this schooling,' he shouted. 'It goes to a girl's head. Actress indeed! Now if she had to do something for a living—which she doesn't, mind—she's got a good enough home and she can stay in it—but if so happen she did have to work, I'd have her do something respectable—in a shop—or the teaching, like you.'

Lyn sat up. She saw light.

'You mean—you think that teaching is respectable—that we seem like respectable girls?'

He looked at her taken aback, and raised his bushy eyebrows. 'Why, yes, miss. I wasn't meaning to be insulting to you—I can see you're nice decent girls, of course—and if you're interested in book-learning—well—'

'You don't think that *we're* painted good-for-nothings?'

'No—no, of course not—'

'You wouldn't mind if Zillah grew up like us?'

'She'll be lucky if she does. I can't see her ever being a sensible young woman, able to speak up for herself.'

'You mean that if she ended up as a "sensible young woman" you wouldn't mind her going on the stage?'

'Impossible! She'd be a skittle-witted hussy by the time she was your age.'

'Mr Pendray,' said Lyn quietly, 'I'm afraid you've been misled by us. We are teaching at the school at the moment, but we are and have been—actresses. We were trained at the British Actors' Guild Academy, and have our own theatre in Fenchester in Fenshire.'

His mouth fell open. 'But—but you're not—professionals, like—are you, miss?' he stuttered.

'Oh, yes,' said Lyn. 'Quite professional. And just as much "sensible young women" as we were five minutes ago.' She rose. 'Well, Mr Pendray, as you feel as you do about our profession, we had better remove our soiling presence from your house,' she said with a smile. 'But I would just like to tell you that if you happen to change your mind and decide to give your daughter a chance, I'm pretty sure she could win a scholarship to the British Actors' Guild Academy in London. At the moment, my friend Sandra here has a younger sister at the Academy. She stays with a very homely and respectable old lady who chaperones her wherever she goes and Zillah could share her digs.' Lyn crossed her fingers behind her back, shuddering at the thought of Mr Pendray seeing the way that Maddy and her little friends ran wild about London. 'And then when your daughter had finished at the Academy, there would always be a place for her in our theatre at Fenchester. One of our mothers would put her up. Our homes are there, you see.'

Mr Pendray seemed to be having difficulty swallowing his apple pie. 'Ay,' he said. 'It's kindly meant, I'm sure...'

They turned to go.

'Goodbye, Mrs Pendray. Thank you for the tea. I'm sorry we've been causing you such a lot of trouble. Goodbye, Zillah. Oh, and by the way, after all this, I suppose you would rather be an actress than stay at home—or work in Woolworth's?'

Zillah looked thoughtfully at them and then at each of her parents in turn. 'Yes, please,' she said at last.

As they walked away down the lane to the main road, Sandra said to Lyn, 'Well, you put on a performance, didn't you?'

'It was terrific,' said Vicky. 'What a pity it didn't do any good. Still we got a good tea—'

Lyn smiled to herself. 'I'm not so sure that it didn't do any good,' she said. 'I bet you that one day in the future we're applying for a job, and a beautiful and soignée creature turns up and cuts us out altogether—and it will be Zillah!'

13

ILL WIND

The following evening when Vicky arrived back at the cottage, she found Sandra sitting by the fire looking worried.

'What on earth's the matter?' she demanded, as she untied her scarf from her head. 'Is there bad news from Maddy?'

'No, it's Zillah. She didn't turn up today.'

Vicky whistled thoughtfully. 'I wonder what's the matter? Do you think her parents have taken her away or anything?'

'I don't know,' said Sandra, 'and I'm worried. I hope they haven't made her leave school altogether. The teacher didn't seem a bit surprised. She says she's always staying away.'

'I wonder,' said Vicky thoughtfully, 'if we should do anything about it? Or have we done our worst already?'

'Let's ask Lynette when she gets in.'

Lyn did not arrive until past eleven, dead tired and very cold, after an infuriating rehearsal and a long bus journey back. When she heard Sandra's news, a determined look came into her eyes.

'We'll go visiting again tomorrow,' she said, and then flopped into bed and fell asleep without discussing the matter further.

The following afternoon they found themselves trudging along the rough lane to the farm once more.

'Do you know,' confessed Vicky, 'I really feel quite frightened in case something awful has happened.'

'But what *could* happen?' said Sandra, trying to be sensible. 'You don't think she's run away—or—or they've locked her up on bread and water, or anything, do you?'

'I don't know,' said Lyn. 'But I just have a feeling that we're needed!'

When they knocked on the door there was a long silence. They were just exchanging worried glances when running footsteps were heard in the house. It was Zillah who opened the door and said, not very welcomingly, 'Oh, it's you—'

'Yes,' said Lynette. 'Is anything wrong?' For Zillah looked worried and dishevelled and almost on the verge of tears. Her face was pale and her nose was very pink. She sniffed miserably.

'Oh, I've got a pack o' trouble...' she complained. 'Mum and Dad are in bed with flu. Dad won't ever have the doctor, but we know it's flu all right. I've got it coming on too, and now the bread won't rise...' She nearly subsided into tears, but sneezed instead.

Vicky and Lynette laughed with relief, and Sandra stepped into the hall and said briskly, 'Now then, Zillah, off you go to bed. What wants doing first?'

Zillah sat back weakly at the foot of the stairs. 'Well, there's the bread needing looking after, and Mum and Dad need their hot-water bottles filled, and they ought to have some tea soon, I suppose—'

'Vicky,' said Sandra in her most 'organizing' voice, 'you take Zillah upstairs and see that she gets to bed all right. Lyn, fill the three hot-water bottles, and I'll see to the bread and get some tea ready.'

Mr and Mrs Pendray were a trifle surprised as they lay in their enormous oak four-poster bed to see Lynette enter the room, untuck the bed-clothes at the foot, collect the stone-cold bottles and exit without a word. But they were feeling too ill to care, and merely grunted their thanks when she returned with piping-hot bottles, carefully wrapped up in little woollen jackets. Vicky had to help Zillah undress, and soon after she was in bed the girl was sleeping a heavy influenza sleep. Down in the kitchen Sandra wrestled with the range, stoking it up with cinders and looking doubtfully at the bread in the enormous oven. After the compact kitchen of her home and the large modern one at her school, this stone-flagged immensity and the large dark pantries and cupboards were a bit bewildering, but she soon found her way around and set out tea on three trays which they carried up to the invalids. Zillah did not waken, so they took hers down again.

'It will do her more good to sleep,' said Sandra. Mr and Mrs Pendray seemed quite glad of their tea, and Mrs Pendray said in a cold-ridden voice that it was 'good of them to help out'.

'Have you got any friends or relations who would come in tomorrow?' Sandra asked. 'Because Zillah has gone down with it now.'

Mr Pendray raised his eyes to the ceiling, and Mrs Pendray sniffed mournfully. 'No, I can't say as we have. There's my sister— but she's a good eight miles away, and she's got six children—'

'Oh, well, don't you worry,' said Sandra. 'We'll look after things as best we can.'

'But what about the milking?' cried Mr Pendray desperately. 'Zillah's gone down now, you say?'

The three girls looked at each other horror-stricken. Sandra saw Lynette open her mouth to say, 'Oh, we can do that—' but Mrs Pendray put in with, 'If you can catch the man before he goes, he'll do it. Tell him Zillah and I can't, and ask him to come early in the morning.' Vicky flew down to the yard, wondering what on earth they would do if 'the man' were gone.

'I'd die if I had to milk a cow,' she thought. But fortunately the farm-hand was still in the stables, and she delivered the message.

'I'll manage, tell the master. Don't 'e worry,' he assured her, grinning cheerfully.

When she got back to the house, she found Lyn and Sandra in conclave in front of the kitchen range.

'We're wondering what we ought to do,' said Lyn.

'Whether we ought to stay here or what—'

'Yes, I think we ought to stay for a few days.'

'But what about our work?'

'I think we could fix it all right,' said Sandra, 'so that one of us at least would be here all the time.'

'You see, Lyn doesn't go out until the evening, and we two are always free after school hours.'

'But would Miss Felton mind?'

'I'll walk to the nearest phone-box,' said Lyn, 'and ring her and see what she says. I'm sure she won't mind.'

Miss Felton was quite definite on the telephone.

'Yes, by all means stay at the Pendrays' for a few days if they really can't get on without you. You can get to your classes just as easily from there as from here, but don't kill yourselves with

143

work, will you? Because, after all, they weren't very pleasant to you the other day, were they?'

'No, but if only you could see what a miserable state they're all in—'

'Very well. You'd better stay then. But mind you don't go down with flu too.'

Sandra knocked gently on the door of Mr and Mrs Pendray's bedroom.

'We're going to stay here tonight, if you don't mind,' she told them. 'Just so that we can get things straight in the morning. Where had we better sleep?'

'There's plenty of spare rooms. Mind you air the beds. Linen's in the chest on the landing—' and Mrs Pendray's voice was lost in an onslaught of sneezes.

'Come on, let's go and choose our rooms.' After struggling with an oil lamp they found out how it worked, and, carrying it in front of them, they started off on a tour of the house. It was terribly dark and draughty and a little frightening, so after inspecting all the rooms they decided for the sake of cosiness they would all sleep in one room, where there was one large bed with an enormous feather mattress, and another smaller bed.

'Then we can light a fire,' said Sandra, 'to air the room a bit.'

The evening passed in a flurry of bed making, fire lighting and preparing supper for the invalids. When they had eaten their supper with many expressions of thanks, Sandra appeared with bowls of warm water and towels.

'Now out you get,' she told Mr and Mrs Pendray firmly, 'and while you're having a wash, I'll make your bed. It looks as though it could do with it.' They seemed unwilling but Sandra was adamant, and when they were settled in their newly made bed again, they admitted they were more comfortable. After dispensing aspirins and banking up the fire, Sandra said goodnight and turned the lamp out.

Downstairs in the kitchen, she said to the other two girls, 'Isn't it amazing how different people are when they are ill? Mr Pendray terrified me the other day, but now he's just like a difficult child.'

'Gosh, I'm tired! Let's have something to eat and get to bed,' said Vicky.

'Yes, I must say this Florence Nightingale act is rather tiring,' yawned Lynette. 'What's in the pantry?' They found a hunk of beautiful creamy cheese and a large jar of pickled onions, which went excellently with slices of the newly baked bread which had turned out quite well eventually.

'Beautifully indigestible,' said Vicky with her mouth full.

As they lay in their strange beds that night, watching the shadows cast on the ceiling by the flickering fire, Sandra said suddenly, 'What on *earth* are we doing here? In a farm miles from nowhere, looking after a horrid old farmer who thinks we're painted hussies, and a girl we're trying to make into an actress—who is so beautiful that she would cut us out any day—'

'Can't imagine,' said Lyn sleepily. 'We seem to have strayed a bit from what we were intending to do, don't we?'

'Yes,' said Vicky, 'but it's quite interesting. I wonder how the boys are getting on,' she added drowsily.

Next morning was not quite such fun. It was freezingly cold when they got up, and the stove had to be relit before they could get any hot water. Vicky, nearly in tears, held a piece of paper in front of the grate to encourage it, wailing, 'And I always thought hot water came out of a tap...'

At last they were washed and dressed and Sandra was frying bacon and eggs. The patients were inclined to be fractious, the mother and father worrying about the state of things on the farm and in the house, and Zillah suddenly realizing that the 'actress ladies' were working like 'skivvies' in her home.

'No, you stay where you are, Mr Pendray,' Sandra said firmly. 'Then you'll be better all the quicker. We're muddling along all right, and the man is looking after everything outside.'

Sandra and Vicky had to go out to their classes next afternoon, so they left Lynette to hold the fort. On returning, to their amazement they found her reading aloud from the Bible to Mr and Mrs Pendray.

'Sh!' she said, as they entered the room. 'This is an interesting bit...' And with great drama she continued the story of David and Goliath. When she had finished Mr Pendray gave a sigh of satisfaction.

'Ay, this young lady can certainly read the Scriptures,' he said.

'Oh, yes, we did a lot of it at Dramatic School,' said Lyn with truth; then added quickly, 'well, I expect you'd like your teas now and I must be getting off to my rehearsal.'

Zillah seemed much better by this time and was anxious to talk.

'Why—why are you doing all this, miss?' she demanded of Sandra, over her tea-tray.

'Looking after you, do you mean?'

'Yes.'

'Well, other people have done things for us—Miss Felton, for instance. So we like to have a chance to do things for other people. And we like you—we're interested in you.'

'But why should you bother about us? You're different sort of folk—you're clever; you're on the stage. Why should you be interested in—in someone the like of me?'

'My dear Zillah, we are very inexperienced, very out-of-work actresses, and we come from families very much the same as yours, except that ours are townspeople, not country people.'

'But what can we do to thank you? And my dad was so rude to you the other day.'

'The best way *you* can thank us is by trying to use your gifts to better advantage than going into Woolworth's—'

Zillah smiled shyly. 'I've changed my mind now. I want to be just like you three are.'

'I hope you'll be a great deal more fortunate than we have been lately,' said Sandra wistfully.

Next day Miss Felton came over to see them, and the farmer and his wife were full of praises for the three girls.

'You've made a conquest here,' Miss Felton told them.

'A very tricky one,' commented Lyn. 'You should have seen our first welcome into the household.'

'Well, how much longer will you be staying here?' asked Miss Felton, 'because I can bring you some more clothes and things over, if you like.'

'No, don't bother,' said Lyn. 'We haven't got much else, have we? And we're only going to be needed here a couple more days.'

The invalids kept up a constant demand to be allowed up, but Sandra told them firmly, 'You can get up the day after tomorrow at tea-time.'

'We'll give them a gala tea,' she told the others, and was up early that morning, baking madly and cleaning everything in the kitchen until it shone.

'Gosh,' grumbled Vicky, as she scrubbed the stone flags, 'let's hurry up and get back into rep. It isn't such hard work.' As it drew near four o'clock, the time that Sandra had told the patients they might get up, she set out on the table the products of the morning's baking. Crisp loaves—the first she had ever attempted—two fruit flans, an apple pie—in fact, a tea identical with the one they had had on their first visit to the farm.

'Honestly, we're not giving the poor beggars a chance,' laughed Vicky. 'What with your Bible reading, Lyn, and Sandra's cooking, they won't be able to enjoy having a good disapproval of us any more.'

'It's a jolly good job Sandra can cook,' said Lyn. 'Can you imagine the muddle we'd have been in without her?'

'My only talents would hardly help matters along, would they?' said Vicky pensively, then burst into a fast can-can round the kitchen.

'Stop it,' hissed Sandra. 'Here they come.'

Rather shyly the Pendrays came in. The girls were touched to see that Mr Pendray had on what was obviously his best suit, with a high starched collar and black tie. Mrs Pendray was wearing the same 'best black' that she had worn at the previous tea-party, and Zillah wore a hideous velveteen dress, which, however, did nothing to destroy the effect of her startling beauty.

'Now you sit near the fire, and don't bother about anything, Mrs Pendray, except to get on with your tea,' said Sandra, picking up the large earthenware teapot. At first there was a little constraint, as sitting round the tea-table like this reminded them all so forcibly of the first time they had all sat there. The Pendrays were obviously afraid that the same subject would be raised, but the girls chatted on about the farm, influenza, the school and even told them the story of how they happened to be with Miss Felton. Zillah listened open-mouthed, laughing occasionally, and then looking doubtfully at her parents to see if they approved. They did approve. Mrs Pendray put in a 'Well, I never...' every now and then, and at the end of their story Mr Pendray slapped the table with his open palm, making them all jump.

'Well, good luck to you, say I. Good luck to you...'

He looked round the room challengingly, as though expecting someone to gainsay him. 'I don't hold with this theatre business, but you're a bunch o' plucky youngsters, I will say that.'

Lyn smiled a satisfied smile and changed the subject.

'Tomorrow,' she said, 'I'm afraid we must leave you and go back to Miss Felton. Now you do all feel well enough to carry on, don't you?'

They assured her of that.

'And Zillah, when will you be back at school?' Sandra wanted to know.

'Tomorrow,' said Zillah promptly.

'Oh, no. Not as soon as that. But by the beginning of next week I should think you'll be all right,' said Sandra. 'In time for the dress rehearsal of the play—'

'Are you excited about going to Edinburgh, Zillah?' asked Lynette innocently.

Zillah looked at her parents and said softly, 'I don't know.'

'She'll have to get rid of that cold before she can go, won't she, Mrs Pendray?' hazarded Sandra. The mother and father looked at each other.

'Indeed she will,' thundered Mr Pendray, intent on being dominant to the last. 'You'll not set foot on the road for Edinburgh, my girl, unless it's better.' And another victory was won.

But the next morning came the real triumph. They were all ready to depart at mid-morning, and were just having a cup of cocoa, and trying to persuade Mrs Pendray not to do too much on her first day out of bed, when Mr Pendray put on his overcoat and announced his intention of walking down the lane with them.

'Oh, no,' cried Sandra, 'there's a terrible cold wind.' But he insisted, and after they had said goodbye to Mrs Pendray and Zillah, he escorted them several hundred yards down the lane.

'You think my girl is a likely girl then?' he said suddenly.

'Very,' said Lynette.

He looked hard at her, then stammered, 'Well—I was wondering, like—if you'd tell me the address of that place, the school place—where you went to...'

After he had left them, they ran the rest of the way down to the main road, chortling with glee, dancing the snow-flake dance in and out of the muddy ruts of the lane.

14

ENCOUNTER

The girls soon began to feel as though they had lived in the country all their lives.

'Wouldn't London seem strange after this?' remarked Sandra, as they walked home along a winding lane one day.

Lyn sniffed at the fresh scent of the air, with an early mist rising. 'D'you know what I'd like to smell at the moment?'

'No.'

'The smell of Leicester Square Underground Station at rush hour. People—and fog—and smoke—and—'

'Lyn!' they shouted her down. 'How disgusting!'

'And I was being so open-air girl...' said Sandra. 'How dare you spoil it.'

But however they felt about it, the country air and wholesome food was doing them a lot of good. They began to get more colour in their cheeks, and Vicky had to make an extra hole in her belt.

'Lenny,' she told the housekeeper, 'your cooking is ruining my waist-line. This can't go on.' And she started getting up earlier in the morning to do a few limbering up exercises.

The three shows that the girls were handling soon began to display a marked improvement, and through teaching, the girls found they were learning a lot themselves.

'I see my cast making mistakes and I tick them off about it, only to realize that I do exactly the same things myself very often,' confessed Lyn.

'And how is your protégée, Sandra?' inquired Miss Felton.

'Fine. She's back at school, and quite recovered, more lively than anyone has seen her before. I've given her a small speaking part that someone dropped out of, and she's doing it very nicely.'

'Good,' said Miss Felton. 'Yes, you've certainly worked wonders in that household.'

'We did everything but milk the cows,' laughed Sandra, 'and I think Lynette was ready to tackle that.'

Miss Skate continued to idolize Lyn. She often invited her back to her bungalow for a cup of coffee while she waited for the bus, and there Lyn would sit helpless under the flow of conversation that gushed from the mouth of her hostess. The bungalow was an absolute museum of knick-knacks, each of which had a long history attached. She had three cats called Pip, Squeak and Wilfred, who sat in the best chairs while their mistress and visitor squatted on hard cane stools. Miss Skate had many other hobbies besides amateur theatricals. She made sprays of artificial flowers which were very popular at the parish bazaars, she informed Lyn, and she also decorated screens with cut-out figures of crinoline ladies in flower gardens. There were piles of books on every piece of furniture, and oddments from her various crafts lay about on the floor.

'Oh, yes, I'm very busy,' she told Lyn. 'There's always something to do. Art is a very claiming companion, as you know. If it's not my flowers it's my screens, and then there are rehearsals most evenings, and I play the organ in church on Sundays. And then I have to keep up my reading, you know, to keep abreast of the times. And also—this is my guilty secret...' she giggled coyly, 'I write a little poetry!'

'Really? How interesting. I should love to hear—'

But before Lynette could finish the sentence the sheaf of scrawled verses had appeared and Miss Skate was reading them aloud in her flutelike voice. They were terrible, and Lyn had to struggle to keep a straight face, but she liked Miss Skate and did not wish to offend her, so when they were finished she said, 'Oh, very interesting. All of them. Most interesting.'

Miss Skate was delighted. 'Oh, you dear creature! You say just the right encouraging word. Other people might say they were beautiful—or pretty—and things like that—but that is not what I'm aiming at. Interesting—that's what I like to hear.'

Lyn returned home in a sober frame of mind.

'Preserve me,' she thought, 'from ever becoming an old fossil like that. But there—I suppose she's happy—happier than most.'

About this time, Miss Skate thought fit to get up a concert in her village, and was very anxious for the three girls to each do a turn.

'It'll probably be agony, but we might as well do our party pieces,' said Lyn to the others.

'I think it will be fun,' said Vicky. 'It's ages since we've done anything like that. I shall dance, of course, but what?'

'Something that's easy to dress,' Sandra reminded her, 'as we haven't got any costumes here.'

'What on earth shall I do?' Lyn wanted to know.

'Recite, I suppose. When people recite at concerts, everyone knows it's because they can't sing or dance.'

'I shall sing something light, and then something religious,' Sandra announced. Finally she decided on a little French song, and Schubert's 'Ave Maria'.

'But *what* shall I wear?' she groaned.

'It's a choice of slacks or tweed skirts,' laughed Lyn.

'If only...' began Vicky, who was about to say, 'If only we were at home,' when she remembered that even had they been at home, their entire wardrobes were in the grubby hands of Mrs Mintey.

'Oh, what shall I dance—' groaned Vicky.

'What was that you were doing in the kitchen at the farm? It looked rather fun.'

'That? Oh, a sort of can-can—yes, I could do it to the can-can from *Orpheus in the Underworld*.' She hummed it under her breath, indicating the dance steps with her fingers. 'But I couldn't possibly dress it... ' Her eyes wandered thoughtfully round the room, and came to rest on a flame-coloured silk lampshade that hung on a standard lamp. It was of beautiful material, and had a gold fringe around the bottom.

'I say,' she cried. 'I wonder if Miss Felton would lend me that?'

'Why, yes,' cried Sandra. 'With white crêpe paper bodice, and petticoats, and long black stockings, and some feathery sort of head-dress, you'd be a real can-can girl.'

Miss Felton was as generous as ever when it came to lending the very lampshade from her lounge. She also lent Sandra a beautiful black evening dress which made her look extremely tall and grown-up.

'Clothes... How lovely they are!' she sighed, sweeping round the room in it, glorying in the feel of a long rustling skirt after weeks of slacks or tweeds.

'But what is Lyn wearing?' asked Miss Felton, turning to where Lyn was sprawled on the floor over a volume of Shakespeare, looking for speeches suitable for recitation.

'Oh, any old thing,' said Lyn. 'Listen, I think I'll do the sleep-walking scene of Lady Macbeth's, and—and a bit of Portia, perhaps—'

'But you can't do it in slacks,' urged Sandra.

'No,' said Lyn vaguely, 'I want some sort of draperies—'

'You shall have them,' promised Miss Felton, and marched out of the room. A second later she was back, carrying a large oyster-coloured velvet curtain that they recognized as belonging to her bedroom.

'The very thing,' cried Sandra and soon the three of them were clustered round Lynette, pinning and draping as though she were a model in a shop window.

'And when I do the Lady Macbeth, I'll put this bit over my head, like this...'

On the night of the concert, they were busy dressing in the tiny little dressing-room of the British Legion hall, when there was a knock at the door. It was Zillah.

'What on earth are you doing here?' said Sandra.

'We've come over for the concert,' she smiled. 'When Dad heard that you three were in it, there was no stopping him.'

'How nice of him,' said Lyn. 'Well, I hope he'll like it.' She looked round the dressing-room.

'Oh, dear...' she said suddenly. Sandra, in the black dress, looked the picture of propriety, but Vicky, who was just suspending her black stockings under her brief frilly skirt, reminded her of Mr Pendray's strict views.

'Vicky!' she cried 'Mr Pendray!'

Vicky looked in the glass. 'Gosh, yes,' she said, 'I look like a painted hussy, don't I? Whatever shall I do?' She wiped off a little make-up, but that didn't seem to help.

'And that dance—oh, Vicky, you can't—it'll just finish off Mr Pendray.'

'I'll tone it down,' declared Vicky.

Zillah looked at her. 'Dad won't like that get-up, I'll warrant.'

They looked at one another in despair. It was almost time for the curtain, and Vicky was the second to appear. It seemed ridiculous to alter her dance just for one member of the audience, but...

'Oh, Vicky...' moaned Sandra. 'And after all the hard work we've put in on Mr Pendray...'

At that moment there was a knock on the door, and one of the helpers came in with a tray of cups of tea.

'Just to encourage the performers,' she smiled. Vicky looked at her as though she was a heavenly apparition. The lady helper was wearing a rather antiquated waitress's garb, with a little starched cap.

'Take off your dress,' rapped out Vicky. The astounded lady was stripped of her grey dress and white collar, cap, cuffs and apron before she could argue.

'Now, Zillah, run out to the accompanist and tell her she is to play my number three times as slowly as we rehearsed it.'

The audience were charmed by the demure little dance of a

red-headed Quaker girl, to a strange slow little tune that no-one connected with anything so frivolous as a can-can.

Mr Pendray clapped and nodded his approval, while a rather bewildered lady helper in a frilly skirt and long black stockings prepared to serve tea.

After Miss Skate's successful concert, the children and grown-ups with plays to perform for the festival set to work in earnest. Lyn, Sandra and Vicky worked hard and long, coaching and encouraging.

As the contest drew nearer, the excitement among the four companies was unbounded. Apart from all thought of the actual competition, the idea of the long journey to Edinburgh was thrilling them. Most of the children had never been more than a few miles out of their native villages, and thought of Scotland as almost a different continent.

Their school teachers took advantage of the situation and taught them Scottish history and geography while their interest was so great. The grown-ups were hardly less excited, and dis-cussed how much luggage they would need for their two days' stay, and what their employers had said when they asked for the time off. The Blue Doors almost wished that they would be able to go up as well, but they knew that this was impossible as they could not afford it. Each week they sent the boys the bulk of the salary that Miss Felton paid them, receiving in return lengthy screeds from the boys, written in Nick's Caff. As there was no news, the letters contained long descriptions of the restaurant and its customers, until the girls could smell the greasy odour of the place, almost hear the clang of the door-bell and the sound of the taxis outside.

'I feel so sorry for them,' said Vicky one day. 'They're trying so hard and getting nowhere.'

'Don't worry,' said Sandra optimistically. 'Things seem to be going on like this for ages, but something will happen suddenly—out of the blue—you'll see.'

'I hope you're right,' said Lyn. 'I wish I could think so.'

As the end of their stay with Miss Felton approached, they began to feel almost frightened. Tumbling straight into a job as they had done made them dislike the thought of trekking off again begging for work. But the search must still be financed, for time was slipping by. It was early Spring now, and the snow-drops that they passed on their journeys had given way to crocuses and the very first primroses. The days of the Blue Door Theatre seemed very far behind them. And then came the final dress rehearsals—chaotic—all of them. Two school children went down with influenza on the eve of the great day, and their parts had to be cut; and at the rehearsal of the adult murder play, a blank cartridge from a pistol exploded too near the leading lady's face, frightening her considerably and singeing her eyelashes.

'Now remember,' were Sandra's last words to her group of children. 'Sing as loudly as you can, except in the places where I've told you to sing very softly, and let them hear your words— and enjoy yourselves, that's half the battle.'

'If anything goes wrong,' said Lyn to her over-excited drama group, 'keep on whatever happens, and try to make out that it's just what you meant to happen.'

'Well,' announced Vicky to the school children, 'Miss Felton and I have done our best. Now it's up to you.'

Next day they had to say goodbye to Miss Felton as she was starting off for Edinburgh for the festival.

'Stay at the cottage as long as you like,' she told them generously. 'Don't rush away unless you want to.'

'We must go,' said Lyn sadly. 'It's been lovely here. But we must move on.'

'Well, Lenny will look after you for a few more days if you want a rest.'

'There isn't time, thanks awfully,' said Sandra. 'And the very *best* of luck. We shall be thinking of you all the time.' Miss Felton shook hands with them warmly and they felt very sad at leaving such a good friend.

'Thank you,' said Sandra weakly, 'for having us.'

'Let me know directly Lucky is caught, won't you?'

'Yes, of course we will. We'll write soon whatever happens.' Into her faithful little car climbed Miss Felton and waved as she drove off. They stood at the gate with Lenny and waved until she was out of sight.

'Ar—she's a good woman,' said Lenny solemnly, as they made their way back to the house.

'She certainly is,' they agreed.

Next day, as soon as they had consumed the enormous breakfast Lenny had prepared for them, they said goodbye to her, and to the little house, and started off. Before she went Miss Felton had advised them to go to a town called Penlannock, in the far west of Cornwall, where, she understood, a small theatre had been started.

'It is run,' she told them, 'by a man named Colin Cowdray. If it is the Colin Cowdray I think it is, I was at university with him. Go and see him and mention me. If it's the same man, he might just help you a bit.' So, with this in mind, the girls decided to get into Cornwall as quickly as possible.

'Penlannock...' said Lyn. 'What a lovely name. I wonder whether we shall work there.'

It was very much warmer than when they had last been on the road, and they were able to take their heavy coats off and walk in their slacks and jumpers. Soon they got their first lift, in a farm lorry, which had a load of baaing sheep in the back. The three girls were crammed in the front, with Lyn on Sandra's knee, and the farmer smoking a strong tobacco that made them cough and splutter so much that they were almost glad when he pulled up and announced that they had reached his destination.

Slowly they made their way westwards, in cars, lorries, roundsmen's vans. Honiton, Exeter, Plymouth, Bodmin, and soon they were in the wild beauty of Cornwall.

Lyn looked across the rolling moors. 'I wouldn't like to get stranded here,' she said. 'Let's get off the road early tonight.'

'Yes,' said Sandra. 'We'll stop at the first hostel we can find in the next town.' This proved to be a hostel for cyclists, and the owner seemed rather surprised to find the three of them turning up at this time of year, and without bicycles. The hostel was empty but for them, and they were allotted little camp beds in a long dormitory. Tired from their journey, they fell asleep instantly.

The following day they reached Penlannock about lunch-time. It was a port on the estuary of a small river, normally a holiday town, but now under the pall of winter-time.

'What a sweet little town,' breathed Vicky, as they stood looking down on it. 'Is that a church or what?' She indicated a large old stone building.

'It's the cathedral—a dear little cathedral,' said Lyn. Already they were in love with the town. It was easy to find the theatre, for there were bills up everywhere directing one to it. It was a small cream-coloured building with photographs hanging outside, unbearably like the Blue Door Theatre. They found the stage door and asked for Mr Cowdray. A bent handsome man appeared and looked questioningly at them.

'Does the name Felton—Constance Felton—convey anything to you?' asked Lynn.

There was a pause as a slow flush mounted to his face.

'Constance!' he breathed. 'Where—how is she?'

'She is very well. She lives near Axminster, and is a Drama Organizer employed by the local Education Committee. She thought you were you, and she sent us to see you.' For a while he seemed too startled at the mention of Constance Felton to pay any attention to the girls, then it seemed to dawn on him that they were asking for work.

'Well,' he said, 'let me see. Next week—yes, I could do with someone to walk on—and also an extra A.S.M. We're doing *Rose without a Thorn*, and I'm playing Henry the Eighth,' he explained. 'I'll take two of you,' he said, and pointed to Lyn and Vicky. 'You to walk on,' he said to Lyn, 'and you to stage manage.'

Sandra said rather pathetically, 'Don't you want someone to sell programmes?'

He looked at her and laughed. 'Oh, you can be a courtier too. But don't expect much money. I warn you.'

They bounded out of the theatre when he had left them.

'We've got some jobs, we've got some jobs,' chanted Vicky. 'Oh, we are lucky girls.'

'Not very good jobs,' grumbled Lyn. 'Now we must find some cheap digs, have a meal and get back to the theatre to lend a hand during the evening show.' They tramped up and down the narrow streets, and eventually found a fisherman's wife in a cottage by the harbour who would take them for thirty shillings a week each.

'We don't even know if we shall be earning that much,' said Lyn, for Cowdray had been vague about money.

It was lovely to be setting out at six-thirty for the theatre. Once more they seemed to have some purpose in life. They lingered outside the theatre, looking at the photographs and revelling in the feeling of belonging again, even though in such humble capacities.

Then they walked into the foyer. Someone they knew was leaning up against the box-office, talking to the girl inside. The angle of the shoulders, the hat, the pointed shoes—they were all familiar. Lyn even opened her mouth to say 'Hallo!' Then he turned to look at them... currant-bun eyes in a rosy face...

'Lucky!' cried Vicky with a scream. In an instant he had shot past them and out into the street. They stood as if paralysed, then turned and followed. But by the time they were outside he had disappeared among the traffic of the busy little harbour.

'He's gone—he's gone—we've lost him...' cried Vicky wildly.

'We must ring Maddy at once and tell her to get the boys down here,' said Lyn.

'Someone you know?' inquired the girl in the box-office.

15

GATHERING IN PENLANNOCK

As soon as the boys had found an empty carriage, slung their grips into the rack and collapsed on to the seats, they began to realize how foolish they had been. As they waited for breath to return, they looked at each other with doubtful eyes.

'What now?' was the unspoken thought in them.

Nigel was the first to come out with it. 'Where had we better ask for when the ticket collector comes round?' he asked grimly.

'Devonshire or Cornwall—that's all we know,' mused Jeremy. 'I'd like to see his face if we said that when he asked us.'

'Oh, we're fools—fools—fools...' cried Nigel suddenly in a rage. 'How can we hope to find him? And now we've let ourselves in for expensive fares—just on a wild goose chase. Cornwall is enormous—it's like looking for a needle in a haystack.'

'Or for Nick's Caff in the West End!' said Jeremy.

'You must remember, Nigel, that Lucky is quite easy to identify. In the country his clothes would cause quite a stir.'

'Not so much of a stir that we shall be able to trace him through two counties.' The train began to gather speed over the tracks, and the sound of the wheels seemed to mock them.

'But what else could we do?' Nigel sounded as though he were arguing with himself. 'We couldn't stay in London knowing for certain Lucky was not there.'

Full of despair they gazed round the carriage, at the dim electric light and the photographs of Cornish beauty spots.

'Sometimes I wonder,' said Nigel, 'if we're a little mad.'

'I've thought that for years,' said Bulldog. 'But what can we do about it?'

'We ought to snap out of it,' said Nigel roughly. 'Stop wasting time looking for a second-rate little thief who has stolen a relatively small sum of money from us, and go about the real business of our lives—being actors, I mean. We seem to have forgotten all about that—lost sight of it altogether.'

'Not lost sight,' objected Jeremy. 'We've just been side-tracked, that's all.'

'Well, we'll lose our way altogether,' said Nigel, 'if we're not careful.' There was a silence but for the wheels, and the derisive hoot of the engine.

'Well—you're the boss—what do you suggest?' said Bulldog, eyeing his big brother with discomfort. 'Get off the train at the next stop? Go back to London and start trekking round the agents? Forget all about the Blue Door Theatre?' Nigel opened his mouth to say something, then shut it again and buried his head in his hands. Bulldog and Jeremy exchanged worried glances. If Nigel were to crack up they would be finished.

'I'm going out for a breath of fresh air,' Nigel said in a muffled voice, and went out into the corridor. The others were too restless to read or to sleep. Out in the corridor Nigel leaned his cheek against the cold window pane, and watched the darkness as it rushed by, wrestling with the thoughts that sped through his over-tired brain. Then someone behind him said, 'Excuse me, sir,' and brushed past him. It was the guard. Immediately Nigel was in action once more. 'I say,' he said, 'I suppose you weren't travelling on this train yesterday?'

'No, sir.' He shook his head. 'No, I wasn't.'

'Oh. Would anyone on this train have been on it last night?'

The guard tilted his cap back and thought a bit. 'Some of the dining-car stewards,' he said finally. 'Yes, they were on.'

Nigel's face brightened. 'Thanks a lot, old man.' It was a different Nigel who opened the door of the compartment and cried, 'Anybody hungry?'

'Of course,' said Bulldog. 'But what's the use?'

'Oh, dear...' Nigel remembered the financial situation.

'We can't all eat—we'll have to toss up.'

'Here, I say,' said Jeremy. 'Do we need a meal? We had some at Nick's before we left.'

'This isn't greed. It's business. Anyone got a coin to toss?' Their pockets were very empty, but Bulldog produced a Dutch coin that had been palmed off on him.

'Odd man out has dinner,' said Nigel. They tossed in turn. It was heads for him and tails for the other two.

'You eat, you wretch,' said Bulldog regretfully. 'But why? That's what I want to know.'

'You'll see later—I hope. Cheerio, wish me good appetite,' and he was gone.

Bulldog tapped his head significantly. 'The strain,' he said.

In the dining-car Nigel seated himself at a table, and tried to catch the eye of the steward.

'What can I get for you, sir?' He was grey-haired and looked tired.

'Were you on this train last night?' Nigel demanded.

The steward seemed surprised. 'Er—yes, sir.'

'Do you remember seeing a young man—about my age—not very tall, with red cheeks, small dark eyes, dark hair greased back, a gaudy tie, probably with something hand-painted on it, and a loudly cut suit?' Nigel watched the steward in agony while he thought.

'I see so many people...' he murmured. 'Wait a minute, sir. I'll ask the head waiter.' A rather more imposing personage was brought forward, and Nigel repeated the description.

'Ah, yes,' said the head waiter. 'No class...' For the minute it did not sink into Nigel's brain that the head waiter had admitted seeing him. Then he jumped on him.

'You mean—you saw him?'

'Yes, sir. I remember him plainly from your description. He was very high-handed with the waiters, but left a large tip.'

Nigel winced, thinking, 'That's a few more shillings of our money...'

'Do you happen to know—where he got off the train?' Nigel's voice trembled with excitement.

'Oh, no, sir. No...' Nigel's face fell. 'I'll ask the other waiters, though. Excuse me.' Nigel could hardly drink his soup for impatience. What with the swaying of the train and the trembling of his hand, most of it went on the table-cloth. Then the head waiter was back.

'Penlannock, sir.'

'Where?'

'Penlannock, he was making for. One of the other waiters remembered him asking which was the best hotel.'

'Penlannock,' repeated Nigel breathlessly. 'That's Cornwall, isn't it?'

'Yes, sir. Just after Truro.'

'Thanks a lot,' said Nigel earnestly. 'I wonder if you would mind leaving me your name and address so that I can send you a token of how thankful I am for your help?'

'Oh, no, sir,' replied the man, smiling. 'If it's as important as that, I'm glad to have been able to help.' And he went off with a friendly smile. But for the fact that he would have to pay for the dinner anyhow, having taken the soup, Nigel would have dashed back to the compartment to give his news to the others. He struggled through the meat and sweet courses but could not wait for coffee. Then he strode back into the compartment where the other two were dozing fitfully. With a gesture he stretched himself out full length on the empty seat opposite them.

'Wake me up at Penlannock,' he said.

The effect of the statement was rather spoiled by the loud hiccup which accompanied it—the result of bolting his dinner.

'Where?' cried the others, sitting upright.

'Penlannock—Queen of the Cornish coast—our Mecca—our Utopia, the hiding-place of our lucky star,' he burbled.

'Talk sense, for goodness sake.'

Nigel pulled himself together. He was really becoming a little light in the head. 'Lucky left the train at Penlannock, a small town in Cornwall,' he informed them; 'and so will we. But it won't be for hours yet, tomorrow morning, in fact. So we might as well get some sleep while we can.'

'Gosh! Gosh!' cried Bulldog. 'It should be easy to trace him there. Do you think—do you think—we're nearing the end?'

'Don't know,' said Nigel shortly, to cover his real feelings. 'We'll see when we get there.'

'Do you realize,' said Jeremy, 'that we shan't even have enough money for a meal?'

'We'll think about that when we arrive,' said Nigel.

'The thing now is to sleep, if we're to be in any state to catch Lucky before we're stranded.' But they were much too excited. Lurid dreams of detection, chasings and captures filled their slumbers. At every station where the train stopped they were jerked into consciousness, and groaned and stretched their cramped limbs. Soon the darkness outside became grey, and then was streaked with red as the sun came up, and by this time the hills of Devon were lit by it. The face of Lucky seemed to float in their dreams, tantalizingly near, yet apt to disappear just as he seemed within reach.

About six o'clock in the morning they gave up all thought of sleep, and sat looking out of the windows.

'Gosh, I'm thirsty,' complained Bulldog. 'What wouldn't I give for a cup of tea—'

'I seem to have the taste of the whole of the British Railways in my mouth,' agreed Jeremy. 'If only we'd known we were coming we could have got a thermos, or rather, a bottle of cold tea like navvies...' They watched the little villages, with their stone houses and red roofs, flitting by, and the never-ending telegraph poles.

'Truro,' cried Nigel excitedly. 'It'll be soon after this. Come on, we must get ready.' Ties were straightened, hair tidied with stubbly ends of combs, and they put on their coats and reached for their shabby grips from the rack. The train slowed up and stopped in the little station of Penlannock. It was small and neat, and had rather the look of a station on a toy railway. There was an early morning atmosphere about it as they stepped out on to the platform which was being swabbed down by a man with a bucket of water. They were the only people to alight, and the train quickly drew out of the station again and disappeared into the cloud of its own smoke.

They looked around them in a lost manner.

'We must start inquiring at once,' said Nigel briskly, and led the way to the hatch of the booking-office where a sleepy clerk was just pushing back the shutter.

'Can I see your tickets, please?' he demanded, and they suddenly realized that they had none. By the time they had paid the three fares, they had one and sixpence halfpenny amongst them. Jeremy and Bulldog looked at the coins, fascinated, but Nigel was attacking the clerk.

'Do you have many Londoners down here?' he inquired.

'Some.'

'Any yesterday?'

'Yes. Good few.'

'Do you remember a young man...' Nigel embarked upon the description of Lucky which seemed to be an exact one, for the clerk's eyes lit up with recognition behind his thick-lensed spectacles.

'Yes, I remember him. Wanted to know the way to the Lion Hotel—that's the best one in the town, y'know.'

'Where is it?'

'Second on the right—you can't miss it.'

169

'Thanks a lot.' And off Nigel hurried.

The other two caught him up. 'But we can't go there, Nigel—not on one and sixpence halfpenny—'

'We must. If we don't find Lucky there, we shall have to work in the kitchen to pay off our bill.'

The streets were narrow and deserted.

'This would be a very pretty little town,' observed Jeremy, 'if my eyes would only stay open long enough for me to look at it.'

'We'll book in at the hotel for a few hours' sleep, then a meal, before we do anything else,' said Nigel.

The girl behind the reception desk of the 'Lion' did not seem at all surprised to have three visitors asking for rooms at that early hour of the morning, as she was evidently used to people coming off the night train. They inquired for Lucky, with the same description, but the girl said, 'Well, I wasn't here yesterday. I only got back from holiday last night. I don't remember seeing the gentleman yet today—what was the name?'

'Green. But I don't expect—'

'No. There's no Green on the register.'

'Oh,' said Nigel. 'Well, we'll look for him in the morning.'

They were shown to two pleasant rooms adjoining each other and looking over the harbour. When the porter had closed the door, Bulldog bounced on the bed to test the springs.

'Gosh, we'll have to pay through the nose for this,' he groaned.

'Lucky will, you mean,' said Nigel determinedly.

'Goodnight, you chaps.'

They slept like logs until lunch-time, then Nigel woke and looked at his watch.

'Hey,' he cried, 'we're slipping. We must get up. Do you realize that at this moment Mr Lucky may be downstairs stuffing his lunch into him.' They tumbled into their clothes, waiting only to splash cold water on their faces and hurried downstairs to the dining-room, peering eagerly round every corner. The dining-room was full, but Lucky was not there. They took a table by the door, and eyed each new arrival.

'It's just like being back at Nick's Caff,' observed Bulldog.

'Except the food's better,' added Jeremy. 'I could do with as long here as we had at Nick's.'

'We'd be in jail by the time it came to paying the bill.'

By the end of lunch Lucky had still not appeared. They questioned the waiter, who was able to tell them that Lucky was definitely staying there, under the name of Halford.

'The nerve!' expostulated Nigel. 'Not content with taking our money, he takes our names.' They fumed for a long time, lying in wait in the lobby, their pent-up tempers rising to boiling point.

'I can't wait here any longer,' cried Bulldog at last.

'Come on. Let's go round the town and look for him. He must be somewhere about if he's still staying at the hotel.'

'O.K.' They set off into the little town, unable to appreciate the smell of the sea, and the cathedral that stood guard above the town. Their eyes darted into every nook and cranny, but there was no Lucky. They walked round Woolworth's and Marks and Spencer's, along the jetty and through an amusement arcade—all the places where they might encounter him—but with no success.

Suddenly Nigel said, 'Hallo, there's a theatre here.'

They studied the bill to which he pointed, and followed the directions on it for reaching the theatre. They turned out of a narrow alley-way and were opposite the small cream-coloured building. And then, to their amazement, out of the door ran Vicky, her red hair flying in the breeze. She went to the middle of the road, looking wildly up and down, and wringing her hands. Behind her in the foyer of the theatre appeared the other two girls.

'Look!' shouted Bulldog, as they stood amazed on the other side of the road. The three girls stood talking with frantic gesticulations, as the boys wended their way across the busy little street.

'What on earth are you doing here?' began Nigel, and Vicky swung round with a cry of surprise. Then she burst into tears on her brother's shoulder.

There was a confusion of questions and explanations, until Lyn shouted urgently at the top of her voice, 'Listen. Lucky was here two minutes ago—he's just escaped. Do you hear? We let him go—we must get a move on—'

'But where—where?' sobbed Vicky.

'The hotel,' shouted Nigel, and led the way. Single file the six of them ran at top speed through the streets of Penlannock, scattering the citizens to left and right.

At the desk the receptionist said brightly, 'Oh, your friend has just this minute left. Paid his bill and took a taxi to the station.'

They turned and made for the station, their breath burning their chests.

'Oh, Nigel—' began Vicky.

'Don't waste your breath,' barked Nigel.

At the booking-office the bespectacled clerk said, 'Oh, that fellow you inquired about this morning has just caught the London train.'

'You mean—he's gone?'

'Yes, the train's just going out now.'

They made a few faltering steps towards the platform, in time to see the tail of the London train swerve round the bend. The clerk looked at their tragic faces, and the tearstains on Vicky's.

'I say,' he called. 'There's a lorry going to London just about to leave from the goods yard. Over there, look. Go and cadge a lift.' They looked wildly at each other.

'Yes, go on,' ordered Lyn. 'We must stay here.'

They ran to the lorry and were aboard it almost before the driver had given his permission.

'Go—to—the—hotel—and—pick—up—our—bags—and—send—them—by—the—next—train—to—Paddington—to—be—called—for—' yelled Nigel, above the noise of the engine.

'Write to us at the Little Theatre,' shouted Sandra.

'Hey,' yelled Bulldog, as the lorry was just moving off. 'We haven't got any money left.'

The girls hastily scrabbled in their handbags and pressed some notes into the outstretched hands.

'Goodbye... Nice to have seen you...' yelled the boys, and the lorry roared off. The three girls, dazed and breathless, stood leaning against each other, looking after it.

'That was so sudden...' said Vicky, with a sob.

16

MAIL BAG

Little Theatre
Penlannock
Cornwall

Dearest Mummy and Daddy

I feel that the time has come for me to write to you to let you know that we are perfectly safe—if not happy. Sandra and Vicky are writing to their parents too. You must have been very worried when you got the notes we left behind us, and we do apologize for the manner in which we have done this. I saw Jeremy yesterday and, although we did not have much time to talk, I can assure you he is all right. So much has happened since we left home over a month ago, that I don't think I can attempt to tell you about it in a letter. I will wait till we are home again, as I pray we shall be very soon. The search for Lucky is taking a very long time, but we are determined to find him. We nearly got him yesterday, but he slipped through our fingers. He won't next time. Of that I am positive.

At the moment Sandra and Vicky and I are working in very unimportant positions at the above theatre, for very meagre sums. The boys have returned to London to continue their chase. If you could find it at all possible to send me some food I should be very grateful—one of your chocolatey cakes, you know... You probably think I don't deserve it after all this, but we are only having bed and breakfast at our digs and trying to economize on other meals, so a cake would help for the teas we brew ourselves in the prop. room.

What is the news of Mr Chubb? Has he recovered properly yet?

All my love to you both, and many apologies for the anxiety we must have caused you. Don't ask us to come home, for we can't till this is all finished,

Your daughter in exile,

LYNETTE

The Cottage
Lukesbury
Nr Axminster

My Dear Girls,

I feel I must write you a line to tell you that my four companies were all placed in the Edinburgh contest. Isn't that wonderful? I must thank you very sincerely for all the valuable help you gave me during your stay, and I would like you to know how very much I enjoyed your company during that time. If you ever wish to come back for a short stay, please do so without even bothering to let me know. Turn up at the door-step and Lenny and I will be delighted.

I do hope your search for work, and the boys' search for Lucky are both meeting with success. Do let me know the latest bulletin, won't you?

I wonder if you got anywhere with Colin Cowdray? I'm sending this care of Maddy at the Academy, so that she can forward it to you.

Perhaps you would like more details of the contest. Sandra's protégées won the cup! A local Edinburgh company came second, Lyn's little bunch came third, mine fourth, and Vicky's were among those honourably mentioned. It is a real triumph for this district, and I have been complimented by the Director of Education. I had to admit that I had received valuable professional advice!

The cottage seems very deserted without you, and there doesn't seem to be much to do now that the contest is over. But still—it will soon be time to start thinking about next year's, I suppose.

Well, keep as cheerful as you were when I met you, and I know things will go your way,

All the best,

Yours sincerely,

CONSTANCE FELTON

PS Lenny sends her love, and when we hear from you will send some cakes.

Dear Mum,

I just bin down Cornwall way. Am back now and hoping to see you soon. Business isn't that good. Not much future in the theatre racket, I should say. Thinking of going in for another line. Hope you are keeping an eye on that box which I left with you last time. I'll be needing it bad soon. So expect me down our way any time. If you could drop a quid to above address should be grateful,

Your loving son,

LUCKY

British Actors' Guild Academy

London WC1

Dearest All,

What jolly rotten luck! I saw the boys last night and they told me. They looked awful, not having washed or shaved for days. For goodness sake hurry up and send their luggage before they get picked up as tramps. Whatever are we going to do now? I wish I could think of something. The boys are in the dumps, and I expect you are. I try hard to be madly cheerful, but it doesn't go down very well. Ah well, I'm used to being sat on. But seriously, things are bad, aren't they? I feel awful staying here, when you're all having a ghastly time. We seem to be just where we started from, only worse, because Lucky knows we're on his trail. He must make a habit of stealing money from box-offices, mustn't he? as that was where he was at Penlannock. I do think he's a pig. Worse than Mrs Potter-Smith. She just talks. He steals.

Well, I've got some lines to learn, so I will have to stop. I'm going out with the boys tonight. We're just going looking. Lucky must be in London somewhere, and if you can bump into him in Penlannock, then we can in Piccadilly. It's hard on the feet though. But still, he may be round the very next corner.

Lots of love,

Yours affectionately,

MADDY

39 *Lower Avenue*
Fenchester

Dear old Lads,

I was very glad to have news of you, via the girls via your parents. They have been extremely worried about you, to say nothing of my humble self. My bronchitis is much better now that the weather is warmer. I went back to bed, you know, with a relapse just after you made your exit. But the landlady has been an angel, and I am doing nicely now and feeling ready for work. I do hope that you either find Lucky and regain the money, or else raise the wind in some other way, so that we can open up again. I am seeing that the theatre is kept clean, and go in every other day to put the heating on so that it will not get damp. Mrs Potter-Smith came to me the other day to ask if she might use it for some monstrosity or other.

I did not quite know what to say, so, knowing that you would wish me to refuse, I told her that we were having the decorators in. If only we were! That made her think, of course, that we were starting up again, and she looked very crestfallen.

Do write again and let me know how you are getting on, and how the chase is progressing. I have heard from Terry at Tutworth Wells, and Myrtle too. They are both straining at the leash to return to us, and say that no other company has the same quality as the Blue Doors, and I agree with them,

With you in spirit,

Your affectionate friend,

EDWIN CHUBB

5 *Linden Grove*
London SE

Dear Lucky-Boy,

Thanks for yours. Glad to hear your alright. Fancy, you bin down Cornwall. Nice, I should think. Sorry about business not being so good. Well, you can come home for a bit and think things over. Yes, I kep that box safe. Some friends called to see you since you bin away. Nice chaps called Jack and Pete and Jo. I told them Nick's Caff but they didn't know it. Still, I expect you seen them by now. Well, all news when we meet. Hope enclosed will help. Hoping this finds you as it leaves

Your loving MUM

Dear Nigel, Jeremy and Bulldog,

We do hope you got back safely on that awful looking lorry. What an extraordinary meeting it was! It would have been lovely seeing you, if only we had had time for a real talk. After you had gone we really began to wonder whether we had dreamed it or not. What a coincidence that Lucky should just pick on the theatre that we are working at! I suppose it wasn't really another coincidence that you should turn up, because you had tracked him down to Penlannock, hadn't you? But, at the time, it seemed just too much. When we got back to the theatre we tried to find out from the girl in the box-office what exactly had been Lucky's approach. She was a local girl who had not been working there long, and she said that he had just dropped in about half an hour before, and had stood talking to her in a way that she said was 'very friendly and nice', and had just asked if he could come inside and warm his hands on the radiator in the box-office. That was when we walked in. A jolly good thing for her that we did! But we could kick ourselves for letting him get away. It was the suddenness of it that did it. He was the last person that we expected to see.

Needless to say, we were in no state to be very brilliant at meeting a new company and lending them a hand backstage that evening! They thought us completely dopey, I believe, but we have made up for it since, and are doing more than our share of work. They are a very nice crowd but terribly *commercial*, somehow, after the Blue Doors. Goodness knows we had to count every penny, but we did have other thoughts than how much money we were making. If only we can start up the Blue Door Theatre again—that is the only thought that is keeping us going. After all the lovely parts we were playing at Fenchester, it is so awful A.S.M.-ing and walking on. It seems we are going backwards instead of forwards.

Still, we mustn't grumble to you, because after all, we at least are in a theatre. Some of them down here had heard of us and have been very sympathetic about our bad luck. But that doesn't really help.

Have you any news of Lucky? What plan of campaign are you following?

We enclose some money, and apologize for it being such a small sum. But we found to our horror on pay day that they are only paying us two-ten each—and our digs come to thirty bob. We do hope you can manage all right on this. It's a pity Maddy's money is so tied up, or you could have borrowed a bit from her.

We have written to the parents at last, so you'll probably be hearing from them. I should think they'll send you some food, too. We told them the situation was rather hungry! We haven't heard from them yet and are hoping they are not too angry with us.

Don't be too depressed. It's difficult not to be, we know, but it doesn't help. After all, it's experience. Sorry to come out with all this good advice but it's becoming a habit with us. We only have to pass each other backstage and one of us says, 'Oh, well, it's a long worm that has no turning,' or 'They say that it's better to travel hopefully than to arrive,' and other helpful mottoes. But seriously, don't get too worried. We can hold out as long as you can and, if the money is not sufficient to see you through, we will look for better paid jobs elsewhere—not in the theatre.

Well, we've got to set the stage for the matinée now, so all the best,

Lyn, Sandra and Vicky

PS Our love to Maddy. Tell her how much we envy her still being at the Academy.

Young Men's Hostel Association
Russell Square, WC1

Dear Females,

Yes, we're back at the above address, a luxurious hostelry, if ever there was one. The warder, or warden, whatever he calls himself, is beginning to get a bit suspicious because we're not working, so we shall soon be slung out, I expect.

What a gay expedition it was to Penlannock! So nice to sniff the sea air for a few moments. It was most strange that we should track Lucky down just when he had encountered you lot. You could have knocked us over with a very small feather when we saw Vicky's red head appearing from the theatre.

The lorry was hardly a joy ride but we made London in very good time, in the early hours of the morning, and returned at once to our favourite hotel, see above, where we were given the bridal suite and caviare for breakfast.

Many thanks for the letter and money. What a shame they are working you so hard for so little. It hardly covers your expenses, does it? let alone ours. But *don't*, whatever you do, give up this job for a non-theatrical one. You're very lucky to have dropped into one all together like this. And we must keep *some* connection with the theatre amongst us.

We're glad you've written to the parents, and sincerely hope they will send us some food. We're down to one (very large) meal a day. Maddy is a brick, and pinches all she can from her lunch at the Academy canteen, but that doesn't go very far.

We haven't had a smell of Lucky, and don't know how to go about it now. We dropped in at Nick's the other night, and he told us that he had seen Lucky and told him that we were looking for him, describing us in detail. Of course, Lucky has not been in since then.

So that's one avenue closed. We've spent a long time standing at the end of Linden Grove, that charming residential neighbourhood, but—no Lucky. We've seen his mother going off to do her shopping, still in her curlers, but have not let her see us. We're doing it in shifts but it's very boring and cold. Don't suppose he'll turn up in Linden Grove—it will probably be somewhere quite unexpected. We were wondering whether to get some part-time work to tide us over, and look for Lucky in our spare time. Bulldog wants to be a sandwich-man, he says, because he's doing so much standing about that he might as well get paid for it.

We are doing our best—please believe that—and as soon as we can we shall stop living on your charity,

So chin up,

Cheerio,

BULLDOG, NIGEL, JEREMY

The Avenue
Fenchester

My dear Sandra,

You are wicked, wicked children! You cannot imagine how worried we all were at your disappearance. I've been imagining the most terrible happenings, but your father, of course, just laughed and said that you'd fall on your feet. I was sure that Maddy knew where you were, but she was as close as an oyster. I'm glad you've found jobs, even though they don't sound very good ones. I'm sorry to hear that you are so hungry and have made a couple of cakes which I will pack up tonight. Mrs Darwin is also doing some baking and Mrs Halford is sending a tuck-box to the boys. Not, of course, that you deserve it, for worrying us all like this.

Oh, why don't you give in and come home and take sensible jobs? I've told you before, we don't mind even if you don't work. There's no need for it. You can be quite useful enough to me about the house. Maddy is quite obviously going to be the wage earner of the family. I don't mean that unkindly, dear, but you are more of a home-bird than she is, aren't you? I just don't see why you should be doing such hard work for so little money, and living in discomfort when you could be having an easy time in your own home. You could keep up your acting as a hobby, and it would be far less worrying than trying to make a profession of it.

But still, I know it's no good trying to argue with you if your mind is made up, so I will just wish you good luck, and pray that the boys may have some success in their search, so that you will be home again soon. We miss you very much, and everyone in the town keeps asking me when you're starting up again as they do miss your plays so much.

Daddy insists on sending you the enclosed blank cheque, just in case you really get into difficulties. Only use it if you must, and don't fill it in for too much, will you?

Give my love to the others, and come home soon,

Your affectionate

MOTHER

PS Do see that your beds are properly aired, won't you? I'm sure you'll catch cold and get really ill. If you should, come home *at once*.

17

THE VALLEY OF DESPOND

The rain came down steadily, uncompromisingly, as if it were determined to continue throughout the day. Nigel and Jeremy, standing in a doorway with their eyes glued on Linden Grove, huddled themselves further into the upturned collars of their overcoats.

'Gosh,' groaned Jeremy. 'Will it ever stop?'

'Never,' replied Nigel.

They were silent for the next hour, each busy with their own bitter and despairing thoughts. Then a bedraggled dripping figure wearing a sodden green hat appeared round the corner, plodding towards them, head down, with the rain squelching in his down-at-heel shoes. It was Bulldog, who had arrived to do his shift and relieve Nigel.

'Post come?' was Nigel's first question as his brother took shelter in the doorway beside him.

'No,' grunted Bulldog. 'And I rang Maddy, but she'd heard nothing either.'

They were anxiously awaiting a letter from the girls, hoping it might contain some more money.

'Then we don't eat tonight,' observed Bulldog.

'No. Not till we've got this week's money. We mustn't eat up the rent.'

They stood in a hungry silence, then Jeremy said, 'There's half that cake of Mother's—don't eat it all before we get back, Nigel, if you're going to the hostel.'

'Yes, I'm going back. Look here, why don't you two come too? It's such a foul afternoon. I'm sure Lucky wouldn't be about in it—'

'But what can we do if we come back—eat a slice of cake and go to bed?' Bulldog clasped his tummy suddenly, 'Ooh!' he groaned. 'There's that pain again.'

Jeremy and Nigel exchanged worried glances. They had been on such short rations for the last few weeks that it was beginning to tell on Bulldog who, being on the podgy side, had more to sustain than they had. He had lost a bit of weight, and complained of cramp in his stomach.

'Come on,' said Nigel. 'We'll all go home and have a binge on the remains of the cake.'

They plunged out into the rain. As they walked, Nigel wrestled with his thoughts, then he said quietly, 'Look, we can't go on like this, can we?'

'The money will probably come tomorrow,' said Jeremy.

'It's not only that,' said Nigel. 'Perhaps the girls are being hungry too.'

There was an uncomfortable pause while they thought about this.

'The way we're going on, we shall be in no condition to deal with Lucky if we ever do find him—much less start rehearsing again.'

'But what else can we do?' demanded Jeremy. 'You were talking about this on the train, and a few minutes later, we got a clue.'

'And a lot of good it did us,' said Nigel. 'No, I think we must soon acknowledge ourselves beaten.'

'And then what?'

'I don't know,' said Nigel, 'and I hardly care.'

The trams and buses rattled and splashed beside them as they made their way up the Walworth Road. The future seemed as bleak as the present, and the old carefree days of the Academy and the Blue Door Theatre seemed as if in another life.

'We'll give it to the end of the week,' said Nigel heavily, 'then we'll give up. I shall go home and let my father find me a job. And if you're wise, you two will do the same.

'Why don't you go on with your music, Jeremy? Start studying seriously again.'

'I should like to,' said Jeremy thoughtfully. 'But do you think that we shall ever be able to settle to anything again?'

'No,' said Bulldog. 'I know I shan't.'

It seemed that whichever side of the road they walked, they were constantly passing food shops. Restaurants that cooked sausages and potatoes and onions in the window, and sent out an aroma that made their nostrils twitch and their mouths water; butcher's shops displaying healthy sides of lamb and inviting steaks; an unattended stall filled with rosy apples and golden oranges made Bulldog dig his hands deeper into his macintosh pockets and say, 'Now I know what starts people pilfering.'

'We'll take a tram when we get to the Elephant,' said Nigel. 'We can just afford it.'

It was luxury to be able to get into the warm steaminess of the tram, and take the weight off their tired wet feet. They were glad the journey to Kingsway took a long time, and sat light-headed and dazed, half asleep in the uncomfortable seats.

Once they were back in the dormitory of the hostel, they fell on the cake and demolished it.

'Delicious,' said Nigel.

'Heavenly,' murmured Jeremy, licking his lips.

'Wish there was a bit more of it,' grumbled Bulldog. 'It's reminded me what eating is like.'

They looked round the deserted dormitory, with the rows of little beds that were all occupied by young men nearly as penniless as themselves. On the wall were drab-coloured pictures of 'The Monarch of the Glen' and vague Scottish lochs. The small windows let in only a filter of light from the heavy rain clouds outside.

'I wish,' said Bulldog, 'that we were at home.'

'We could be,' said Nigel.

Thoughts of roaring fires and large meals and loving parents filled the cold dormitory, and they huddled in misery on their beds, wrapped in the thin rugs, while the light faded. They soon decided that it was warmer in bed and before they had been long between the coarse sheets they were mercifully asleep, but restless and ill at ease. When the noise of the other occupants preparing for bed brought him to consciousness later in the evening, Nigel woke up and thought to himself very clearly, 'This must stop. At the end of the week we shall go home.' And then, comforted by the thought that his mind was now made up, he turned over and slept more easily.

Next morning they rang Maddy at the Academy directly after breakfast.

'Yes,' she announced cheerily; 'the letter's come and I think it's got some money in it. It feels lumpy. I'll give it to you this evening. Can you last out till then?'

'Well—er—no. Not really.'

'O.K. then. I'll meet you for lunch. Will you come to Raddler's?'

Raddler's was the little café round the corner from the Academy where all the students congregated.

'No, Maddy. We look too shabby—even for Raddler's.'

'Don't be such stooges. Still, we'll make it the Help Yourself, if that's how you feel.'

Breakfast at the hostel had been sparse and not at all filling, and they looked forward all the morning to the prospect of loading their lunch trays with everything that was going. They spent the time wandering round all the back streets of Soho with a weather eye open for Lucky. Although they passed coffee shops where they were sure he must sometimes drop in to meet a friend, and newsagents whom they were sure he must patronize for his sporting papers, he was as invisible as ever.

Maddy was waiting for them at one o'clock and she gasped when she saw them. 'What have you been up to? You look terrible. What have you been doing?'

'Nothing. Not even eating much,' confessed Jeremy. Purposefully Maddy walked away. 'Hey! Where are you going?'

'Come with me.' She led them back into Soho, to Chez Bertrand, a tiny shabby restaurant, famous for its cooking.

'You're having lunch with me today.' In spite of their protests she insisted on ordering an enormous and delicious meal, and the four of them fell on it with relish.

'It's an excuse for me to eat a lot too,' she told them, as they got to the apple tart and ice cream.

'But we can't let you pay for this—'

'Well, if you pay for it out of the little that the girls have sent you, you won't have any left. So it looks as if you'll have to let me pay, doesn't it?'

Over coffee Nigel suddenly said, 'Maddy—you'd better know. We're giving it up at the end of the week.'

Maddy looked blank. 'Giving what up?'

'The search.'

'You mean—for Lucky?'

'Yes.'

Maddy stared at each of them in turn as though she could not believe her ears. 'You're not serious?'

'Yes. We're killing ourselves like this. And the girls too. It's getting us nowhere. Even if we did find Lucky now, we wouldn't have the strength to deal with him.'

Maddy's blue eyes slowly filled with tears. 'So—what will happen to Blue Door Theatre?'

Nigel shrugged. 'It belongs to the Town Council, you know. Not us. They'll probably let it out for amateur shows.'

'Mrs Potter-Smith prancing about on *our* stage...'

Suddenly Maddy put her head down on the table and started to cry properly. The boys looked round the restaurant in embarrassment. 'How *can* you let us be beaten like this?' she sobbed; 'after all that's happened. We've done so much— and now...'

The three boys patted her clumsily on the back and said, 'Now, now,' rather feebly, but they were feeling hardly more cheerful themselves.

The waiter eyed Maddy questioningly, and asked if he could fetch her anything.

'No, thanks,' said Nigel. 'She'll be all right.'

Soon Maddy's despair turned to anger. 'I always thought you were so marvellous,' she told them bitterly. 'I used to wish you were my brothers, not just friends, and I used to envy Vicky and Lynette for having brothers when I'd only got a sister, but now I'm glad. I couldn't bear to hear any brother of mine talking like that—'

'But Maddy, dear,' said Nigel. 'I don't think you quite realize what these last few weeks have been like. It's been all right for you at the Academy—you've been safe and warm and well fed—but it has been extremely hard for us, and I expect, for the girls. As a matter of fact, it won't hit you so badly as us if the Blue Door Theatre never opens again. You've got all your film connections to fall back on when you leave the Academy.'

Maddy looked at him steadily. 'And you think that should make up for the loss of the Blue Door?'

'No. Not make up for it—but you'll be able to make a living.'

'And that was all the Blue Door meant to you—a living?'

Nigel shuffled in his chair. 'No. It meant everything. And now we've lost everything, and we might as well admit it.'

Maddy bounced with vehemence. 'But we haven't; we haven't! While Lucky is alive we've still got a chance to get back our money. Oh, why am I tied up in this wretched Academy? I bet you if I were looking for him I'd find him.'

'Don't be a little silly,' said Bulldog curtly. 'Do you think you can do more than we have?'

'Yes.'

'What?'

'Not give up.'

'Maddy,' said Jeremy quietly, 'if you had not been good enough to buy this meal for us, I should throw the remains of this roll right in your stubborn little face.'

'I'm glad I'm stubborn,' shouted Maddy, going pink with feeling; 'you've got to be stubborn. How else should we ever have done anything if we hadn't been? And now is the time to be stubborner than ever.'

'Yes,' said Bulldog, 'it's all right to say that on a full stomach.'

Maddy turned on him. 'I wanted to come with you, you know I did, and risk an empty stomach, but you wouldn't let me. And now you're talking as though I never wanted to—'

'Sh! Maddy! He doesn't mean it like that,' Nigel tried to calm her. 'We're *glad* you haven't had to put up with anything.'

'Well, *you* can be finished with the search if you like,' said Maddy, 'but I shall go on looking for Lucky till the end of my days.'

Bulldog gave a shaky smile. 'I can just imagine you a very tiny little old woman, livid with rage, hobbling up to a very seedy old man and saying, "Are you Lucky Green?" and going "Clonk" with her umbrella.'

Maddy tried hard not to laugh, and looked very stern, but the corners of her mouth turned up and she laughed aloud with tears still in her eyes. 'You are a fool, Bulldog. I'm sorry I made such a spectacle of you.'

'That's all right. But I think we'd better go now. The waiters are beginning to look a little uneasy as to what might happen next.'

Outside, Maddy said, 'But I mean all that. I think you're being rotten to give up, and I never shall. You'll be ashamed of yourselves when I capture Lucky single-handed.'

The boys reflected. Yes, it would be rather shaming but totally impossible.

'All right, Maddy. You keep up the search. But only in your spare time, mind. We'll give it to the end of this week.'

'But what about the girls?' Maddy wanted to know. 'Are you sure that they're ready to give up?'

'I think they will be when they realize just how bad things are with us.'

Maddy shook her head regretfully. 'This isn't the gang I've been used to. What's the matter with you? Have you grown up, or something?'

Nigel said sadly, 'I think that must be it.'

They walked back nearly to the Academy, but left Maddy before they reached the square, as they could not bear to see the building to which they had carried so many dreams and ambitions. When Maddy said goodbye, she added, 'I bet you something will turn up during this week to make you change your minds. A clue, or something.'

'It's this being without any clue whatsoever that is so terrible,' said Nigel. 'That's what made us see how hopeless it is.'

'You'll see,' said Maddy. 'Something will turn up. I'll think of something.'

Thinking had never been Maddy's strong point, in fact her teachers had been used to saying, 'Use a little thought Maddy, do...' But for the next week she thought solidly and logically. She thought on the way to the Academy, so that buses and taxis had to swerve to avoid her blind crossing of streets. She thought all during lessons, so that her notes were always very brief and far from the point. She even thought during rehearsals, and missed her cues and entrances so that she had one of her best parts taken away from her. And she even thought during her meal-times, and merely toyed with her food, which was most unusual for Maddy. All her friends noticed it and teased her.

'What's the matter with Maddy?' cried Buster. 'Why the tragedy queen act?'

'Shut up,' Maddy said tersely. 'I'm thinking. Can't you see that?'

'Oh, is that what it is! I knew you were in pain of some kind.'

And this is how her train of thought went, 'Lucky is a thief. He makes his living going round theatres, especially fairly new ones being run by not very experienced people, and gets friendly with whoever is in the box-office. Now, is that his usual method of making a living? Well, we know of his doing it twice, so there's every chance of his doing it again. Now how does he know where to go? Well, he must read *The Stage* and find out where there are new companies. But could one trace him through that? No, he wouldn't be a regular subscriber to the paper, he'd just buy it at any newspaper stand. But I might try inquiring at all the newspaper shops and stands that sell it—there aren't so very many of them. But that's no real clue. I must think of something to stop the boys giving up...'

All day and far into the night she racked her brain that was not used to such constant use, but it was not while she was engaged in consciously 'thinking' that she eventually found her inspiration. It was during the rehearsals of *Othello*. She was playing Desdemona in the death scene, and was being purpose-fully smothered by a determined young Moor from Kennington. For the first time for days, Maddy was concentrating on what she was doing—which was keeping enough of the pillow out of her mouth to say her last few lines. Suddenly, just as she was at length supposed to be dead, she electrified the class by leaping off the couch with a wild gaze, and shouting, 'Yes—yes, of course...' Othello looked terrified, and wondered if he had hurt her.

'Maddy, what *is* the matter?' demanded the Shakespeare teacher. But the only answer was the slam of the door behind Maddy's flying figure.

18

AMBUSH

Down the marble staircase, flight after flight, she ran. She entered the telephone-box, panting for breath, and feeling in her pocket for coppers.

'I want to send a telegram,' she announced breathlessly when the operator answered her, 'to—to Halford, Young Men's Hostel Association, Russell Square, WC1. The message is: *Have got an idea. All may be saved. Meet me tonight.* And the signature is—*S. Holmes.*'

'Beg pardon?'

'S—for Sherlock—Holmes.'

She could not wait to have the message read back to her, but dashed up the stairs again and back to the class, where she resumed her position on the couch as though nothing had happened.

'Maddy! What *was* the meaning of that?' Maddy looked at her instructress so reproachfully that the good lady coloured and said, 'Well, you must ask permission another time.'

The time until the classes were over seemed endless, and then she was afraid that the boys might not have received the wire in time. But when she ran out of the swing doors there were three familiar figures skulking round a nearby corner, their hats at a despondent angle. With pigtails flying, her arms full of books and face shining with excitement, she ran up to them.

'Well?' said Nigel, not very encouragingly.

'An idea...' she panted. 'I've got one. A wonderful one. The obvious one! Now, listen—'

'Wait a minute,' Nigel interrupted. 'We can't stand here and talk. We shall keep seeing people we know. Let's go and sit somewhere quiet.'

They found a secluded seat in the square between two bushes, and the boys sat down.

Maddy stood facing them, jigging with excitement.

'When you hear you'll kick yourselves for not thinking of it before,' she told them gleefully.

'Well, come on, let's have it,' growled Bulldog. 'It's sure to be some cock-eyed scheme.'

'You remember,' said Maddy, 'what we did when we first wanted someone to look after the box-office? We advertised in *The Stage*, didn't we? And do you remember what a funny collection of people turned up? Then we got Mr Chubb.'

'Well, what about it?'

'We know that Lucky makes a point of picking on new companies and getting in with them. Well, why don't we put a nice inviting advertisement in *The Stage* that will attract him. You know, something like "Energetic young business manager and box-office secretary wanted by new company." Something that would just catch his eye.' The three boys began to sit up.

'I'm pretty sure he reads *The Stage*—yes, he used to buy it every week—I remember plainly.'

'And you—you think he'd answer it?' said Nigel slowly.

'He might, mightn't he? And there's no harm trying.'

The boys looked at each other with hope dawning in their eyes.

'We—we were going home the day after tomorrow—' said Jeremy uncertainly.

'Oh, all right,' said Maddy casually. 'I expect I can manage it by myself.'

'But what—what would we do if he *did* answer?' asked Bulldog. 'Put the police on him?'

'No,' said Maddy, her eyes sparkling. 'We'd arrange a meeting somewhere, and—and confront him. After all, you boys have been saying for months what you'd do when you found him.'

They looked a little shamefaced. Then Nigel said, 'Maddy, you've got something.'

They looked at her admiringly. Jeremy slapped his knee.

'Just *fancy* us not thinking of that before! All these weeks...'

Maddy giggled delightedly. 'I told you you'd be livid. Now are you going home?'

'Of course not,' said Nigel briskly. 'This throws an entirely different light on things. I'll go and put the advertisement in tomorrow.'

'No, you won't,' said Maddy. 'I shall. It was my idea.'

'Oh, well—shall we come too?'

'Mm—yes,' Maddy allowed. 'But don't try and make out it was your idea, will you?'

'No,' said Nigel meekly.

'What had the advertisement better say?' said Jeremy, producing pencil and paper.

They scribbled out several drafts before they finally decided on: *Wanted, enterprising young man for box-office and management of newly formed theatre company. Must have experience, and accept full responsibility for business side.*

'That'll get him,' said Maddy, clapping her hands delightedly, 'and we'll give him a box number, and he'll never guess it's us.'

'We'll take it to the office the first thing tomorrow morning,' said Jeremy, 'and then it will be just in time for next week's issue.'

'I'll have to cut a class and come with you,' said Maddy. 'It'll be History of Drama. Mrs Siddons will have to get on without me.'

Next morning they went along to the office of *The Stage* and were there as soon as it opened. They spread out on the counter the piece of paper with the advertisement on, and Maddy said, 'Please, we want to put this in this week's issue.'

'Sorry,' said the man behind the counter. 'We're all full up. It'll have to wait until next week—or even the week after...'

Their faces fell visibly.

'Is it urgent?' the man asked quite kindly.

Maddy drew a deep breath. 'Yes,' she said. 'You see, it's like this...' And with no more ado she proceeded to tell him the whole story of Lucky, and the predicament they were in. The torrent of words, and the sincerity of the emotion with which she told the story, seemed to daze him slightly. She had talked for quite five minutes, when finally she finished up with, 'And so, you see, it's a matter of life and death.'

'I see...' said the man faintly. 'It is urgent, you might say. Well, I'll try and squeeze you in. It'll mean leaving someone else out, but I'm sure they wouldn't mind if they heard your story.'

'May you be rewarded,' said Maddy grandly, and sailed out of the office.

Bulldog wiped his brow. 'Whew,' he said; 'Maddy, you could talk the tentacles off an octopus.'

'And now,' said Maddy, 'all we have to do is wait.' The days of waiting were terrible. At times it seemed certain that Lucky must answer the advertisement, at others it seemed ridiculous to suppose that he would fall into their trap. Maddy could not concentrate on her studies, and the boys did not even bother to go out looking for Lucky. One night they were even so rash as to go to the cinema, spending a few more shillings of the last of their money.

'If he doesn't answer,' said Nigel afterwards, as he slid into the narrow hostel bed, 'we really have had it. We shall just have to go home.'

'He *must* answer,' said Bulldog between clenched teeth.

'Why should he?' demanded Jeremy. 'At this moment he is probably happily engaged in swindling some poor wretched company somewhere. He doesn't need to waste stamps answering advertisements. So why should he?'

Bulldog flung a pillow at him to relieve his feelings.

The week-end passed slowly. They wandered round all day Saturday, and on Sunday morning went to church at St Martin's-in-the-Fields, feeling rather shabby among the smart congregation.

Maddy became more and more depressed. 'Perhaps it wasn't such a good idea after all. When will you go home?'

'Tuesday, I should think, if we've heard nothing from the advertisement.'

'Have you told the girls? And the parents?'

'No. Not yet.'

On Monday morning the boys were just sitting down to their uninviting breakfast in the dining-hall of the hostel, when one of the officials came up to Nigel.

'Oh, Halford,' he said. 'Your—er—sister's waiting in the lobby to see you. She seems distressed.'

'Vicky?' cried Nigel, jumping up. 'Whatever's up?'

The three of them hurried out into the lobby. The official had been wrong. It was Maddy. She was stretched out luxuriously on the hard wooden form in the hall-way with a blissful smile on her face, and large tears were rolling out of her eyes.

'Maddy—'

'A letter...' She sat up and waved a sheet of paper at them, clutching in her other hand a pile of envelopes. Nigel and Jeremy pounced on it in silence, while Maddy and Bulldog danced a wild fandango to the amazement of the other young men on their way out to their shops and offices.

Dear Sir, ran the letter, which was written from the Linden Grove address. *In answer to your advert in 'The Stage' I beg to apply for the post. I am twenty-five years of age, and have had much experience of the type what you are needing. I have been manager for Red Radcliffe and his Rhythm Boys, also in several West End theatres. Should be glad to call whenever convenient. My references are spotless. Yours truly, L. Green*

'Spotless!' cried Bulldog 'Gosh, he'll be far from spotless when we've finished with him.'

They ran out into the sunlight of the street and up the road.

'Where are we going to?' panted Maddy.

'Don't know,' said Bulldog, 'but we must go somewhere.'

'Let's ring the others and tell them to come up to town at once.'

'Yes. There's a phone-box down there. Oh,' said Nigel, 'no money.'

'Reverse the charges,' said Maddy wisely.

It seemed ages before they got through to the Little Theatre at Penlannock, and centuries before the girls were brought to the phone. Then 'Hallo!' said Lyn's voice from very far away.

'Lyn—' Maddy shouted in the receiver excitedly.

'Maddy! What on earth do you mean by reversing the charges?'

'It's urgent,' gabbled Maddy. 'Come up to town at once. It's Lucky.'

'They—they haven't *got* him?'

'No—but we're going to. And you must be here. Come up to town tonight. It'll be tomorrow.'

'What will be?'

'The grand capture, of course.'

'What on earth are you talking about?'

'Here, Nigel,' said Maddy, 'you take over. They won't believe a word I say.'

Nigel took the receiver and said briskly, 'Hallo, you! I think it will be a good thing if you came up to town tonight. Things are about to happen.'

'Really?' Lyn's voice throbbed with excitement.

'Where shall we come to?'

'Well, you can't come to our place. Better go to Maddy's digs. She'll tell you about it.'

'O.K. See you tomorrow.'

When they came out of the phone-box they did not quite know what to do next, but Nigel said firmly, 'Now this needs thinking out. Where's a good place to think?'

'Somewhere near food,' said Maddy promptly. 'I was too excited to eat any breakfast.'

'First,' said Nigel, 'we'll go to a post-office to send a telegram to Mr Green, requesting his presence tomorrow morning.'

'Where?'

'I don't quite know. It must sound feasible—'

'I know,' cried Bulldog. 'Let's hire a rehearsal room. They're quite reasonable. We'd only need it for an hour.'

'And what an hour it will be—' breathed Nigel.

'Gosh, we've just *got* to get him this time...' breathed Bulldog.

The Locarno rehearsal rooms were in a little alley-way off Leicester Square, appropriately named 'Ranting Yard'. It was a shabby grey building, with each floor divided into two large bare rooms where, for a few shillings an hour, companies could rehearse plays, or with the aid of an out-of-tune piano, variety acts could rehearse their numbers. The door-keeper sat on a little canvas stool outside the entrance with a large ledger in which he entered how long each room was occupied, and who paid him how much. When the Blue Doors arrived in full force the following day the whole building was shaking with the beat of a swing band that was rehearsing in the top front. On the floor below, a soprano warbled 'Ah, Sweet Mystery of Life', and on the ground floor, a chorus were tapping out a fast routine to a tinkly piano.

'Bit noisy today, sir,' said the door-keeper cheerfully to Nigel.

'You've said it. But we shan't mind. In fact... Oh, my name is Holmes. I've engaged a room from eleven till twelve.'

The door-keeper consulted his ledger. 'Oh, yes, sir. Top back. Here's the key.'

Behind Nigel came Bulldog and Jeremy, looking tense but determined. Then came Maddy, in a state of uncontrollable excitement. Vicky, Lyn and Sandra, pale and heavy-eyed from their all-night journey, walked together arm-in-arm, and behind them, a giggling seething bevy, were the six ex-pantomime fairies, Buster and her gang.

'Oh, I'm expecting a young gentleman by the name of Green a bit later on. Will you send him up?'

'Yes, sir.'

Nigel turned to Maddy and the six little girls. 'I shan't want you lot until Green arrives.' He winked at them surreptitiously.

'Yes, Mr Holmes,' said Buster loudly, pink with excitement under her freckles. 'We'll be about...'

Maddy led the cortège along the side of the building farthest away from the main road, but one snub nose was kept just peeping round the corner.

The Blue Doors mounted the stairs in silence.

'Oh, dear,' said Sandra. 'Supposing...' But she was in too bad a state to be able to think what catastrophe she was fearing.

Nigel unlocked the door. It was a large bare room with chairs round the walls and a table at one end. Nigel seated himself in front of the table, facing the door.

'Girls,' he said, 'you sit round the table behind me. Jeremy and Bulldog behind the door.' They grouped themselves as he ordered. 'Now just supposing he gets away—don't worry. He won't get far.'

Sandra said anxiously, 'I hope Maddy will be all right.'

'She'll be fine,' Jeremy reassured her. 'This sort of thing is right up her street.'

'It's eleven o'clock,' said Lyn tensely, looking at her wrist watch. They were silent, watching the blackness of the door.

'Aah—sweet mystery of life,' wailed the soprano.

'Boom-boom-de-boom, boom-boom-de-boom, Alexander's Rag-time Band...' thudded the orchestra. And the dancers tapped madly to the tune of 'The Dicky Bird Hop'.

Lyn's heart was pounding so loudly that it seemed to her to be shaking her whole body. She thought that she had never cared so violently about anything in her whole life.

'Gosh, that piano's flat,' said Jeremy softly, not relaxing his listening attitude. Then they heard footsteps—loud confident footsteps that mounted the uncarpeted wooden stairs.

'Here he is,' hissed Jeremy. 'I know those steps.'

'Oh! Oh, dear...' cried Sandra helplessly. 'Whatever will happen?'

'We mustn't let him go,' said Bulldog.

'We won't,' said Nigel confidently.

The steps seemed to get louder, louder than the piano, the soprano, the dancers—louder even than the swing band. And yet the brusque knock on the door made them all jump. For a minute no-one could answer, then Nigel shouted in a very stern voice, 'Come in.'

The door swung open and there stood Lucky.

He was dressed in a new chocolate-brown pin-striped suit, with a yellow waistcoat and a flaunting orange tie. His black patent shoes were shinier than ever, and so was his hair. His cheeks were pink and so well washed that they were shining. His wide-brimmed hat was held in front of him. While the door still swung open he stepped across the threshold and opened his mouth to speak. But although his mouth stayed open, no words came.

Nigel met his horrified gaze levelly. 'Hullo, Lucky,' he said; 'so you want a job in a box-office, do you?'

'Funny, eh?' Lucky gave a sickly chuckle and Jeremy and Bulldog moved from behind the door to close in on him. But suddenly his wits returned to him, and like an eel, he turned and slithered between them. Bulldog flung himself at his feet in an unsuccessful rugger tackle, Jeremy grabbed at his shoulders and received a blow on the jaw that sent him reeling. The three girls screamed, and by the time that Nigel was across the floor, Lucky was out of the door and gone.

'Get him, get him!' shouted Nigel. Jeremy and Bulldog picked themselves up and were after him in a flash, with Nigel behind them. They fell, rather than ran, down the top flight of stairs, shouting strange battle cries at the top of their voices. 'Stop thief!' and 'Catch him!' and 'Look out, Maddy!' By the time they reached the bottom of the flight, Lucky was descending the next flight. In the doorway out into the street, the six fairies and Maddy were playing innocently with a skipping rope. The door-man was turning one end and Buster the other, while Maddy bounced up and down over the rope, singing out, 'Salt, Mustard, Vinegar, Pepper...' But they each had one eye on the staircase. As Lucky's flying figure appeared on the stairs, Maddy snatched the handle of the rope from the door-man.

'O.K., Buster,' she yelled, and they pulled the rope taut. Out of the door came Lucky, as fast as his legs would carry him.

'Hooray!' yelled the fairies, as he tripped helplessly over the rope and crashed on to the ground. They were on to him in an instant, sitting heavily on his head, his legs, his feet.

In vain he kicked and writhed. By the time the others arrived scarcely any of Lucky was visible. Nigel had to clear them away from the prostrate form to reach the victim.

He held Lucky by the scruff of the neck and said threateningly, 'Well, let's have it! Where's our money?'

Lucky was snuffling unashamedly. 'At 'ome,' he said. 'My mum's lookin' after it.'

19

CURTAIN CALL

Fenchester station was seething with life. There was a small crowd standing on the platform watching the line, and the photographers from the two local papers were walking up and down importantly with their cameras. Mr and Mrs Fayne, Mr and Mrs Darwin and Mr Halford stood chatting together round the wheel-chair of Mrs Halford, who was flushed with excitement and looking prettier than ever. The Mayor and one or two of the Councillors were having a word with the station-master, inquiring how late the train would be. Myrtle, in a new hat, Terry and Mr Chubb, Ali and Billy, paced up and down impatiently, smiling with relief and excitement, shouting and talking sixteen to the dozen.

For the Blue Doors had hit the headlines. Nobody quite knew how it had happened, but a reporter had appeared like magic on the scene of the scuffle outside the rehearsal rooms and, scenting an original story, had written them up in several columns of the 'London Gossip' page of the evening paper. There was also a very bad photo of them, all looking very dirty and untidy, as indeed they had been at the time it was taken, with all their names in the wrong order underneath so that it read 'Maddy' for 'Bulldog' and vice versa, much to their indignation.

There had been a violent exchange of telegrams between the Blue Doors and their parents, and the exiled members of the company, but the most important wire of the lot was the one that Nigel sent to Mr Chubb: *Money regained. We open in a fortnight. Begin preparations. Back tomorrow.*

And so now Fenchester was out in full force to welcome them back, and as the train appeared like a toy in the distance, a murmur ran through the crowd and Mrs Halford dabbed her eyes with a lace handkerchief.

'A bit different from the way we skulked out of the town...' remarked Nigel, leaning from the window and waving. As they stepped on to the platform there were exclamations of surprise, for never had the Blue Doors looked so smart. Fenchester was used to seeing them off stage in their oldest and untidiest rehearsal clothes. But, true to his word, Nigel had insisted that the first thing they did with the money must be to replenish their wardrobes.

'It's not extravagant,' he said. 'We shall be needing clothes for the coming season.' So the next day had been a gorgeous 'squander', as Maddy called it. And they certainly looked a different collection of beings now. Gone were the slacks and jumpers, the macintoshes and boots. Sandra was wearing a black suit that showed up the fairness of her hair, Vicky had a deep mauve swagger coat, and Lynette a wine corduroy dress and jacket. The boys had compromised by buying new sports coats and pressing up their old trousers.

'We'll all have new suits when we can get them fitted at leisure,' Nigel had promised.

Maddy had come off worst as she had not sold any clothes in the first place. But to keep her happy they had let her have a new hat—a red stockinette monstrosity with a long dangling tassel.

The parents were the first to reach them, and there was terrific embracing and kissing, and 'You *naughty* children!' exclaimed in loving tones. The photographers flashed their cameras, intent on brightening up the sober pages of the Fenshire papers.

'Good for you!' cried Nigel to Mr Chubb, as the first thing he saw on the platform was a large bill saying in enormous letters, *Blue Door Theatre, Grand Reopening, April 3rd.* The Mayor came forward and shook hands with them heartily.

'Trust him,' murmured Maddy. 'He knows he's going to have his money back before long.' It took ages for everyone to get shepherded into the correct cars and taxis, and when at last they were all packed in, the vehicles were directed to the Halfords' house where tea for the whole party was to be served in the large lounge.

After many cakes had been consumed and second cups of tea drained, and no-one had really had a chance to talk sensibly to anyone, Mr Fayne said, 'Look here—we don't really know what's happened at all. I'm sure the newspapers gave a very garbled account of it. Maddy can't possibly have tripped him up with a skipping rope—'

'I jolly well did!' said Maddy proudly. 'Didn't I? He came a lovely cropper.' She giggled at the recollection.

'But—how did you *get* him there?'

They explained about the decoy advertisement and the rendezvous at the rehearsal rooms.

'And what did you do with him after you caught him?'

'Well,' said Nigel, 'I suppose we were rather silly. We ought to have handed him over to the police. But we didn't. You see we'd met his mother, and she was a sweet old thing—and—well, somehow we just couldn't. So we made him take us down to Linden Grove where he lives, get the money and hand it over to us. Then we gave him ten minutes to get away, and then rang the police and told them we'd recovered our money and they could do whatever they chose about Lucky.'

'I hope they continue to look for him,' said Mr Darwin. 'After all, he may go on robbing other companies.'

'I fancy not,' said Nigel. 'I think he was quite shaken at being shown that he couldn't always get away with it.'

'I wonder why he hadn't spent the money,' mused Mr Chubb.

'He said he'd been waiting a bit, in case the police had any way of checking up on the notes.'

'Well, they hadn't. How could they? He might just as well have spent it.'

'Thank goodness he didn't,' sighed Lyn. 'Oh, we have been lucky.' She smiled contentedly round the room.

'And what are we opening with?' Mr Chubb wanted to know.

'The show we were rehearsing when we closed down,' said Nigel, and immediately he and the manager were engaged in a long conference about business details.

Suddenly Mrs Fayne cried, 'Maddy—I've just thought. What on earth are *you* doing here? You should be at the Academy still. Term isn't over yet, surely?'

'Not for another week,' said Maddy calmly, 'but Mrs Seymore said I'd better come home too, because I was so excited I wouldn't be any use for anything for the next week. So I came.'

Mrs Darwin admired the brand new raw hide suitcases that the Blue Doors had also invested in. She picked one up and said, 'Oh, they're very light, aren't they?'

'Would you like to see what's in mine?' inquired Bulldog.

'Yes—it doesn't feel as though there's much—'

'There's not,' he chuckled. Inside the case when he opened it were three dirty rain-stained out-of-shape hats—one green, one grey, one brown—with sadly drooping brims.

Ceremoniously, Bulldog picked his up between finger and thumb and dropped it gently into the fireplace.

'Look out,' cried Nigel; 'it'll put the fire out.' It almost did, and created such a ghastly smoke that the other two boys merely took theirs outside and dropped them into the dustbin.

'Gosh! How wonderful to see the end of those...' cried Jeremy.

Mr Chubb was searching through his pockets. 'I had some telegrams somewhere—ah, here we are...' He handed three orange envelopes to them. 'They came to the theatre this morning.' All were merely addressed 'Blue Doors'. The first read: *Congratulations on the success of your search. Good luck for reopening, Constance Felton.* The second read: *How dare you walk out on me. You are sacked. Know you'll be glad, as have read papers. Good wishes, Cowdray.* And the last read: *Please ring John Blomfield, Theatre Newsletter Programme, BBC, re live broadcast from your theatre.*

Nigel read and reread this several times, then gave a shout of triumph.

'Hey—listen to this!' He read it aloud.

'Fame at last!'

'Quick!' cried Maddy. 'Go and ring up at once!' Nigel dashed to the telephone in the hall and dialled Trunks. In the lounge there was a fresh hubbub of excitement. Nigel reappeared at last, flushed and a little dazed.

'It's all fixed,' he told them. 'They want us for the "Curtain Call" item in their programme. You know, it's a different company every week. They do a bit out of a show—and then are interviewed about themselves. Well, the night we reopen they want to broadcast the last ten minutes of the show, and then interview us for another ten. Isn't that super?'

Before he had finished speaking, Mr Chubb was at the phone passing the glad news on to the local papers, and arranging for special bills with 'Broadcast performance' across them in large letters.

'Dear Mr Chubb seems to have found a new lease of life since his illness,' remarked Sandra. 'Now he's almost as much of a live wire as Lucky was.'

'Funny...' remarked Lyn. 'Do you know, Lucky may have done us a good turn after all. He's certainly given us a nice little spot of publicity, hasn't he?'

'Just the sort he would have loved.'

'It means that his little racket is at an end,' said Bulldog.

'Once we've broadcast the story, everyone will recognize the description of him if he ever tries it on again.'

'Oh, isn't life wonderful,' sighed Vicky, stretching luxuriously on the couch and looking round the room. 'And isn't it heavenly to be home. I've never appreciated it so much before.'

'Yes, it's super,' agreed Maddy, surreptitiously reaching out a hand for the remaining brandy snap that lay looking lonely on the plate.

'Maddy!' said her mother, noticing this; 'you're not in your own home yet.'

'Let her have it,' laughed Mrs Halford. 'If she doesn't, Bulldog will.'

Bulldog smiled peaceably. 'Yes, it's good to be home to be nattered at again,' he said.

By now everyone had outstayed the polite time for an invitation to tea, and eventually the Faynes and Darwins departed, but not before Nigel had announced loudly and joyfully, 'Rehearsal tomorrow—ten o'clock.'

'What a wonderful prospect—work again,' sighed Jeremy. 'I'll never again grumble at having to rehearse. Not after all those awful weeks of not being an actor, but being a detective—and not a very good one at that.'

They shouted goodnights up the road as they departed, and then the three houses closed their doors and their curtains, but there were lights in the windows until very late that night as each of the families went over the children's adventures and thanked heaven for their home-coming.

The Blue Door Theatre was packed to capacity, with as many people standing at the back as regulations would allow. The opening performance of *Granite* was approaching its end. The dour drama had been unfolded to a breathless audience that only stirred to applaud at the end of the acts. Lyn was giving the performance of her life, and it looked as if it were going to be the best thing that they had ever done. The news that the tail end of the show was to be broadcast had spread far and wide, so for that performance they could have filled the theatre three times over.

'Silly, aren't people?' observed Maddy; 'when the whole point of the wireless is that people can sit at home and hear things.'

All day a BBC mobile van had been at the theatre, fitting up mikes and instructing the Blue Doors as to what they were to do. A short script for the interview had been prepared from notes taken down by Mr Blomfield during conversations with the seven of them, and they rehearsed it several times.

'Don't sound so miserable,' he kept telling them. 'This is one of the happiest days of your life, isn't it?'

'Yes, of course,' said Lyn. 'Don't we sound like it?'

'No. You sound as though you're at your own funerals. Buck up a bit and talk naturally, like you did when we first met.' They soon overcame their microphone nerves and began to rattle away like their true selves.

The parents had been undecided whether to stay at home and listen over the radio, or whether to come to the theatre. Eventually, the Faynes and Darwins came to the theatre and the Halfords stayed at home, as it was easier for Mrs Halford.

The climax of the play approached, and suddenly a little red light flashed on at the side of the hall. That meant that they were on the air, and that not only Fenchester, but the whole of the world could hear them. It was a terrifying thought, and made Vicky's throat go dry and croaky. But Lynette began consciously to concentrate on the light and shade in her voice, and not to think so much of her movements. She strived to keep within a sensible range of the mikes, as the BBC man had instructed. And she knew she was being good. There was an admiring glint in the eyes of the other characters on stage as she embarked on a long speech, and in the audience a pin could have been heard if anyone had wished to drop one. Then the end of the play arrived and they were all taking the curtain, bowing and smiling. The applause was immense but it immediately subsided when Mr Blomfield raised his hand. Drawing them into a group round the mike, he read from the script, 'You have just heard the closing few minutes from the play *Granite* by Clemence Dane, from the Blue Door Theatre, Fenchester, and now I have pleasure in introducing you to the young artistes, most of them well under twenty, who have performed it. Well, Blue Doors—how are you feeling this evening?'

'Wonderful'—'Terrific'—'Glorious'—were their replies as they hastily found their places in the scripts that an assistant was handing them.

'You see,' continued Mr Blomfield, into the mike, 'tonight is a very special occasion in the annals of the Blue Door Theatre. And Nigel Halford, the director of the company, and quite an old man compared to the others, will tell you why.'

Nigel, very hot round the collar, was led to the mike. For a moment of sheer panic he wanted to say, 'No, thank you. I'd rather go home to bed,' but then he heard his own voice, clear and assured, saying, 'A few months ago it looked as if the theatre that we had dreamed of for so many years, and finally opened, was fated to close before it had run for many months...' And slowly, with many scripted interruptions from the others, the whole story of the Blue Door Theatre was unfolded. At the story of the tripping up of Lucky with the skipping rope, the audience laughed, and the Blue Doors had to pause for a bit until Mr Blomfield signalled them to continue.

'And so, you see,' Nigel wound up, noting with relief that he was on the last page of the script, 'everything has come right in the end. With the money retrieved we can pay off our debts and start again. The last few months have seemed long and very trying, but I think we must all admit that they have added to our experience of life, and to our determination to continue with this venture. Don't you think so?' he addressed the others.

'Yes,' said Lyn, 'although I wish it had never had to happen. Yet I know that I, for one, appreciate the opportunity to have our own company in our own home town all the more for having lost it for a while.'

'Well, thank you, Blue Doors. I feel sure that all the listeners will join with me and the audience here in the theatre, in wishing you every success in the future, and congratulating you on your efforts in the past. Goodbye, Lynette, Sandra, Maddy, Vicky, Bulldog, Jeremy, Nigel and the rest of the company. Goodnight...'

The red light flashed green, and everyone relaxed as the curtain fell upon more tumultuous applause.

'Very nice,' said Mr Blomfield. 'You sounded almost as happy as you look. And the show was magnificent.' He turned to Nigel, 'My goodness, you've got one little actress who knows what she's doing, haven't you?'

'We certainly have,' said Nigel.

'Can you keep her with you, though?' he wanted to know.

'I think so.'

'Well, you need never want for work, any of you. If ever you get the broadcasting bug, just let me know, and I'll try and put in a good word for you here and there.'

'That's jolly kind of you, sir. Come and have some sandwiches.'

The parents had brought sandwiches and coffee to be consumed in the dressing-rooms, as they knew it would be ages before their children would be ready to go home. The tiny dressing-rooms were packed with congratulating friends and relations just as at other Blue Door first nights, but tonight the local press was present again, the Director of Education was trying to inquire when they would be able to put on something for school-children's matinées, and the producer from a theatre in a neighbouring town was trying to discuss a possible exchange system, whereby they would play one fortnight in Fenchester and the next in the other company's theatre, twenty miles away. But Nigel would not talk business. He threw a quite good-natured temper tantrum.

'I'm not discussing anything tonight,' he said. 'Come and see me here tomorrow morning—or else write to me. Too much has happened lately. I'm just a limp rag—can't think straight.'

The parents tactfully withdrew, encouraging as many other people as they could to do the same. Ali and Billy cleared up the stage and set it for the next night's show, and with Myrtle and Mr Chubb and Terry called out cheery 'Goodnights' and went home. Only the seven of them were left at last, lazily taking off their make-up in adjoining dressing-rooms. Maddy hummed a little tune. They were all too tired to talk much.

'Doesn't seem as though we've ever left here, does it?' observed Lyn with a yawn.

'Just like any other first night.'

'Only better,' said Maddy. 'Broadcasting and that—'

'It went beautifully,' sighed Sandra. 'Think how many thousands of people must have heard it—'

'Think how many people will be writing to ask for jobs—' shouted Nigel from the next-door dressing-room.

'It'll be a nice change from us looking for jobs,' said Vicky.

'I wonder,' said Sandra, 'if we're here for the rest of our lives?'

'I wonder.' Lyn gazed at her reflection in the mirror, dark eyes with heavy tired shadows under them.

'Do you mind if you are?' demanded Nigel from the next room.

Lyn put her head on one side and considered it, and her reflection did the same. Did she? At one time she would have recoiled from the thought of doing any one thing for the rest of her life—but now, after the last few months...

She looked round the untidy little room where Maddy, Sandra and Vicky, half stripped, sat among the litter of grease-paint and costumes. In the next room Bulldog was singing tunelessly under his breath, and Jeremy could be heard splashing and spluttering under the water tap.

'Well?' repeated Nigel.

'No,' shouted Lyn. 'I don't mind.'

'O.K. Coming?' yelled Bulldog, as he yelled every night when he was ready to go home. There were the same old 'Wait a minute' and 'Coming now' and 'Come *on*, Maddy,' and then they were ready to switch out the last lights, dash back for things they had forgotten, and eventually were all outside and the door locked. It was a lovely night, warm and still, with a little crescent of moon just beginning to appear over the roof tops.

'I'm tired,' said Maddy, in an enormous yawn. They linked arms.

'What a night...' breathed Vicky. 'I'll never forget it.'

'I say,' said Nigel, 'you remember in the second act when I entered, and you weren't down left, Jeremy, as you should have been...'

220

And there they were again, on the usual post-mortem, of who had done what, right and wrong, during the show.

Off they went down the road away from their theatre, silhouetted like cardboard figures—three quite tall, three a bit shorter and one on the dumpy side—disappearing into the dusk of the Spring night.

THE END

THE ADVENTURE CONTINUES IN
Maddy Again

PUSHKIN CHILDREN'S

Maddy Again

By the author of
The Swish of the Curtain

PAMELA BROWN